BOOK ONE

DEEP BLUE

JENNIFER DONNELLY

Dısnep • HYPERION

LOS ANGELES   NEW YORK

All rights reserved. Published by Disney·Hyperion, an imprint of Disney
Book Group. No part of this book may be reproduced or transmitted in any
form or by any means, electronic or mechanical, including photocopying,
recording, or by any information storage and retrieval system, without written
permission from the publisher. For information address
Disney·Hyperion, 125 West End Avenue, New York, New York 10023-6387.

Printed in the United States of America

First edition
10 9 8 7 6 5 4 3 2 1
G475-5664-5-14046

Library of Congress Cataloging-in-Publication Data
Donnelly, Jennifer.
Deep blue/Jennifer Donnelly.—First U.S. edition.
pages cm.—(Waterfire saga; book 1)
Summary: Uncovering an ancient evil, Serafina, a mermaid of the
Mediterranean Sea, searches for five other mermaid heroines who are
scattered across the six seas, to save their hidden world.
ISBN 978-1-4231-3316-2 (hardback)
[1. Mermaids—Fiction. 2. Supernatural—Fiction. 3. Magic—Fiction.
4. Good and evil—Fiction.] I. Title.
PZ7.D7194De 2014
[Fic]—dc23   2013049105

Endpaper maps and chapter opener illustration by Laszlo Kubinyi

Reinforced binding
Visit www.DisneyBooks.com

SUSTAINABLE FORESTRY INITIATIVE   Certified Sourcing
www.sfiprogram.org
SFI-00993

THIS LABEL APPLIES TO TEXT STOCK

DEEP BLUE

For Daisy,
with all my love

For more than once dimly down to the beach gliding,
Silent, avoiding the moonbeams, blending myself with the
shadows,
Recalling now the obscure shapes, the echoes, the sounds and
sights after their sorts,
The white arms out in the breakers tirelessly tossing,
I, with bare feet, a child, the wind wafting my hair,
Listen'd long and long.

—From "Out of the Cradle Endlessly Rocking,"
by Walt Whitman

PROLOGUE

DEEP IN THE black mountains, deep in the Romanian night, deep beneath the cold, dark waters of the ancient Olt, the river witches sang.

> *Daughter of Merrow, leave your sleep,*
> *The ways of childhood no more to keep.*
> *The dream will die, a nightmare rise,*
> *Sleep no more, child, open your eyes.*

From her place in the shadows, the elder, Baba Vrăja, watched the blue waterfire, her bright eyes restive and alert.

"Vino, un rău. Arată-te," she muttered in her age-old tongue. *Come, evil one. Show yourself.*

Around the waterfire, eight river witches continued their song. Hands clasped, they swam counterclockwise in a circle, their powerful tails pushing them through the water.

> *Daughter of Merrow, chosen one,*
> *The end begins, your time has come.*

The sands run out, our spell unwinds,
Inch by inch, our chant unbinds.

"*Vin, diavolul, vin,*" Vrăja growled, drawing closer to the circle. "*Tu esti lângă . . . te simt. . . .*" *Come, devil, come . . . you're near . . . I feel you. . . .*

Without warning, the waterfire rose, its flames licking out like serpents' tongues. The witches bowed their heads and tightened their grip on one another's hands. Suddenly one of them, the youngest, cried out. She doubled over as if in great pain.

Vrăja knew that pain. It tore inside like a sharp silver hook. She swam to the young witch. "Fight it, dragă," she told her. "Be strong!"

"I . . . I can't. It's too much! Gods help me!" the witch cried. Her skin—the mottled gray of river stones—paled. Her tail thrashed wildly.

"*Fight it!* The circle must not break! The Iele must not falter!" Vrăja shouted.

With a wrenching cry, the young witch raised her head and wove her voice once more into the chant. As she did, colors appeared inside the waterfire. They swirled together, coalescing into an image—a bronze gate, sunk deep underwater and crusted with ice. A sound was heard—the sound of a thousand voices, all whispering.

Shokoreth . . . Amăgitor . . . Apateón. . . .

Behind the gate, something stirred, as if waking from a long sleep. It turned its eyeless face to the north and laughed.

Shokoreth . . . Amăgitor . . . Apateón. . . .

Vrăja swam close to the waterfire. She shut her eyes against the image. Against the evil and the fear. Against the coming bloodred tide. She dug deep inside herself and gave all she had, and all she was, to the magic. Her voice strengthened and rose above the others, drowning out the whispering, the cracking of the ice, the low, gurgling laughter.

> *Daughter of Merrow, find the five*
> *Brave enough to keep hope alive.*
> *One whose heart will hold the light,*
> *One possessed of a prophet's sight.*
>
> *One who does not yet believe,*
> *Thus has no choice but to deceive.*
> *One with spirit sure and strong,*
> *One who sings all creatures' songs.*
>
> *Together find the talismans*
> *Belonging to the six who ruled,*

Hidden under treacherous waters
After light and darkness dueled.

These pieces must not be united,
Not in anger, greed, or rage.
They were scattered by brave Merrow,
Lest they unlock destruction's cage.

Come to us from seas and rivers,
Become one mind, one heart, one bond.
Before the waters, and all creatures in them,
Are laid to waste by Abbadon!

The thing behind the bars screamed with rage. It hurled itself against the gate. The impact sent shockwaves through the waterfire into the witches. The force tore at them viciously, threatening to break their circle, but they held fast. The thing thrust a hand through the bars, as if it wanted to reach inside Vrăja and tear out her heart. The waterfire blazed higher, and then all at once it went out. The thing was gone, the river was silent.

One by one, the witches sank to the riverbed. They lay on the soft mud, gasping, eyes closed, fins crumpled beneath them.

Only Vrăja remained, floating where the circle had been. Her wrinkled face was weary, her old body bent. Strands of gray hair loosed from a long braid twined like eels around her head.

She continued the chant alone, her voice rising through the dark water, ragged but defiant.

> *Daughter of Merrow, leave your sleep,*
> *The ways of childhood no more to keep.*
> *Wake now, child, find the five*
> *While there's time, keep hope alive.*
>
> *Wake now, child, find the five*
> *While there's time, keep hope alive.*
> *Wake now, child . . .*

ONE

"WAKE *UP*, CHILD! Suffering Circe, I've called you five times! Have you sand in your ears this morning?"

Serafina woke with a gasp. Her long, copper-brown hair floated wildly around her face. Her eyes, darkly green, were fearful. That thing in the cage—she could still hear its gurgling laughter, its horrible screams. She could feel its cunning and its rage. She looked around, her heart pounding, certain it was here with her, but she soon saw that there was no monster in her room.

Only her mother. Who was every bit as terrifying.

"Lolling in bed today of all days. The Dokimí is tonight and you've so much to do!"

La Serenissima Regina Isabella, ruler of Miromara, was swimming from window to window, throwing open the draperies.

Sunlight filtered through the glass panes from the waters above, waking the feathery tube worms clustered around the room. They burst into bloom, daubing the walls yellow, cobalt blue, and magenta. The golden rays warmed fronds of seaweed anchored to the floor. They shimmered in the glass of a tall gilt mirror and glinted off the polished coral walls. A small green octopus that had been curled up at the foot of the bed— Serafina's pet, Sylvestre—darted away, disturbed by the light.

"Can't you cast a songspell for that, Mom?" Serafina asked, her voice raspy with sleep. "Or ask Tavia to do it?"

"I sent Tavia to fetch your breakfast," Isabella said. "And *no*, I can't cast a songspell to open draperies. As I've told you a million times—"

"Never waste magic on the mundane," Serafina said.

"*Exactly*. Do get up, Serafina. The emperor and empress have arrived. Your ladies are waiting for you in your antechamber, the canta magus is coming to rehearse your songspell, and here you lie, as idle as a sponge," Isabella said. She batted a school of purple wrasses away from a window and looked out of it. "The sea is so calm today, I can see the sky. Let's hope no storm blows in to churn up the waters."

"Mom, what are you doing here? Don't you have a realm to rule?" Serafina asked, certain her mother had not come here to comment on the weather.

"Yes, I *do*, thank you," Isabella said tartly, "but I've left Miromara in your uncle Vallerio's capable hands for an hour."

She crossed the room to Serafina's bedside, her gray sea-silk gown swirling behind her, her silver scales gleaming, her thick black hair piled high on her head.

"Just *look* at all these conchs!" she exclaimed, frowning at the pile of white shells on the floor by Serafina's bed. "You stayed up late last night listening, didn't you?"

"I had to!" Serafina said defensively. "My term conch on Merrow's Progress is due next week."

"No wonder I can't get you out of bed," Isabella said. She picked up one of the shells and held it to her ear. *"The Merrovingian Conquest of the Barrens of Thira* by Professore Giovanni Bolla," she said, then tossed it aside. "I hope you didn't waste too much time on *that* one. Bolla's a fool. An armchair commander. He claims the Opafago were contained by the threat of sanctions. Total bilge. The Opafago are cannibals, and cannibals care nothing for decrees. Merrow once sent a messenger to tell them they were being sanctioned, and they ate him."

Serafina groaned. "Is *that* why you're here? It's a little early in the day for a lecture on politics."

"It's *never* too early for politics," Isabella said. "It was encirclement by Miromaran soldiers, the acqua guerrieri, that bested the Opafago. Force, not diplomacy. Remember that, Sera. Never sit down at the negotiating table with cannibals, lest you find *yourself* on the menu."

"I'll keep that in mind, Mom," Serafina said, rolling her eyes.

She sat up in her bed—an enormous ivory scallop shell—and stretched. One half of the shell, thickly lined with plump pink anemones, was where she slept. The other half, a canopy, was suspended on the points of four tall turritella shells. The canopy's edges were intricately carved and inlaid with sea glass and amber. Lush curtains of japweed hung down from it. Tiny orange gobies and blue-striped dragonets darted in and out of them.

The anemones' fleshy fingers clutched at Serafina as she rose. She pulled on a white sea-silk robe embroidered with gold thread, capiz shells, and seed pearls. Her scales, which were the bright, winking color of new copper, gleamed in the underwater light. They covered her tail and her torso, and complemented the darker copper shade of her hair. Her coloring was from her father, Principe Consorte Bastiaan, a son of the noble House of Kaden in the Sea of Marmara. Her fins, a soft coral pink with green glints, were supple and strong. She had the lithe body, and graceful movements, of a fast deep-sea swimmer. Her complexion was olive-hued, and usually flawless, but this morning her face was wan and there were dark smudges under her eyes.

"What's the matter?" Isabella asked, noticing her pallor. "You're as white as a shark's belly. Are you ill?"

"I didn't sleep well. I had a bad dream," Serafina said as she belted her robe. "There was something horrible in a cage. A monster. It wanted to get out and I had to stop it, but I didn't know how." The images came back to her as she spoke, vivid and frightening.

"Night terrors, that's all. Bad dreams come from bad nerves," Isabella said dismissively.

"The Iele were in it. The river witches. They wanted me to come to them," Serafina said. "You used to tell me stories about the Iele. You said they were the most powerful of our kind, and if they ever summon us, we have to go. Do you remember?"

Isabella smiled—a rare occurrence. "Yes, but I can't believe *you* do," she said. "I told you those stories when you were a tiny merl. To make you behave. I said the Iele would call you to them and box your ears if you didn't sit still, as a well-mannered principessa of the House of Merrow should. It was all froth and seafoam."

Serafina knew the river witches were only make-believe, yet they'd seemed so real in her dream. "They were *there*. Right in front of me. So close, I could have reached out and touched them," she said. Then she shook her head at her foolishness. "But they *weren't* there, of course. And I have more important things to think about today."

"Indeed you do. Is your songspell ready?" Isabella asked.

"So *that's* why you're here," Serafina said archly. "Not to wish me well, or to talk about hairstyles, or the crown prince, or anything *normal* mothers would talk about with their daughters. You came to make sure I don't mess up my songspell."

Isabella fixed Serafina with her fierce blue eyes. "Good wishes are irrelevant. So are hairstyles. What *is* relevant, is your songspell. It has to be perfect, Sera."

It has to be perfect. Sera worked so hard at everything she did—her studies, her songcasting, her equestrian competitions—but no matter how high she aimed, her mother's expectations were always higher.

"I don't need to tell you that the courts of both Miromara and Matali will be watching," Isabella said. "You can't afford to put a fin wrong. And you won't as long as you don't give in to your nerves. Nerves are the foe. Conquer them or they'll conquer you. Remember, it's not a battle, or a deadlock in Parliament; it's only a Dokimí."

"Right, Mom. *Only* a Dokimí," said Serafina, her fins

flaring. "*Only* the ceremony in which Alítheia declares me of the blood—or kills me. Only the one where I have to songcast as well as a canta magus does. Only the one where I take my betrothal vows and swear to give the realm a daughter someday. It's nothing to get worked up about. Nothing at all."

An uncomfortable silence descended. Isabella was the first one to break it. "One time," she said, "I had a terrible case of nerves myself. It was when my senior ministers were aligned against me on an important trade initiative, and—"

Serafina cut her off angrily. "Mom, can you just be a *mom* for once? And forget you're the regina?" she asked.

Isabella smiled sadly. "No, Sera," she said. "I can't."

Her voice, usually brisk, had taken on a sorrowful note.

"Is something wrong?" Serafina asked, suddenly worried. "What is it? Did the Matalis arrive safely?"

She knew that outlaw bands often preyed upon travelers in lonely stretches of water. The worst of them, the Praedatori, was known to steal everything of value: currensea, jewelry, weapons, even the hippokamps the travelers rode.

"The Matalis are perfectly fine," Isabella said. "They arrived last night. Tavia saw them. She says they're well, but weary. Who wouldn't be? It's a long trip from the Indian Ocean to the Adriatic Sea."

Serafina was relieved. It wasn't only the crown prince and his parents, the emperor and empress, who were in the Matalin traveling party, but also Neela, the crown prince's cousin. Neela was Serafina's very best friend, and she was longing to see her. Sera spent her day surrounded by people, yet she was always lonely. She could never let her guard down around her court or her servants. Neela was the only one with whom she could really be herself.

"Did Desiderio ride out to welcome them?" she asked.

Isabella hesitated. "Actually, your father went to meet them," she finally said.

"Why? I thought Des was supposed to go," said Serafina, confused. She knew her brother had been looking forward to greeting the Matalis. He and Mahdi, the crown prince, were old friends.

"Desiderio has been deployed to the western borders. With four regiments of acqua guerrieri," Isabella said bluntly.

Serafina was stunned. And frightened for her brother. "What?" she said. "When?"

"Late last night. At your uncle's command."

Vallerio, Isabella's brother, was Miromara's high commander. His authority was second only to her own.

"Why?" Sera asked, alarmed. A regiment contained three thousand guerrieri. The threat at the western borders must be serious for her uncle to have sent so many soldiers.

"We received word of another raid. On Acqua Bella, a village off the coast of Sardinia," Isabella said.

"How many were taken?" Serafina asked, afraid of the answer.

"More than two thousand." Isabella turned away, but not before Serafina saw the unshed tears shimmering in her eyes.

The raids had started a year ago. Six Miromaran villages had been hit so far. No one knew why the villagers were being taken, or where, or who was behind the raids. It was as if they'd simply vanished.

"Were there any witnesses this time?" Serafina asked. "Do you know who did it?"

Isabella, composed now, turned back to her. "We don't. I wish to the gods we did. Your brother thinks it's the terragoggs."

"The *humans?* It can't be. We have protective songspells against them. We've had them since the mer were created, four thousand years ago. They can't touch us. They've never been able to touch us," Serafina said.

She shuddered to think of the consequences if humans ever learned how to break songspells. The mer would be hauled out of the oceans by the thousands in brutal nets. They'd be bought and sold. Confined in small tanks for the goggs' amusement. Their numbers would be decimated like the tunas' and the cods'. No creature, from land or sea, was greedier than the treacherous terragoggs. Even the vicious Opafago only took what they could eat. The goggs took everything.

"I don't think it's the humans," Isabella said. "I told your brother so. But a large trawler was spotted in waters close to Acqua Bella, and he's convinced it's involved. Your uncle believes Ondalina's behind the raids, and that they're planning to attack Cerulea as well. So he sent the regiments as a show of strength on our western border."

This was sobering news. Ondalina, the realm of the arctic mer, was an old enemy. It had waged war against Miromara—and lost—a century ago, and had simmered under the terms of the peace ever since.

"As you know, the Ondalinians broke the permutavi three months ago," Isabella said. "Your uncle thinks Admiral Kolfinn did it because he wished to derail your betrothal to the Matalin crown prince and offer his daughter, Astrid, to the Matalis instead. An alliance with Matali is every bit as valuable to them as it is to us."

Serafina was worried to hear of Ondalina's scheming, and she was surprised—and flattered—that her mother was discussing it with her.

"Maybe we should postpone the Dokimí," she said. "You could call a Council of the Six Waters instead, to caution Ondalina. Emperor Bilaal is already here. You'd only have to summon the president of Atlantica, the elder of Qin, and the queen of the Freshwaters."

Isabella's troubled expression changed to one of impatience, and Serafina knew she'd said the wrong thing.

"The Dokimí can't be postponed. The stability of our realm depends upon it. The moon is full and the tides are high. All preparations have been made. A delay could play right into Kolfinn's hands," Isabella said.

Serafina, desperate to see approval in her mother's eyes, tried again. "What if we sent another regiment to the western border?" she asked. "I listened to this conch last night . . ." She quickly sorted through the shells on her floor. "Here it is—*Discourses on Defense*. It says that a show of force alone can be enough to deter an enemy, and that—"

Isabella cut her off. "You can't learn to rule a realm by listening to conchs!"

"But, Mom, a show of force worked with the Opafago in the Barrens. You said so yourself five minutes ago!"

"Yes, it did, but that was an entirely different situation. Cerulea was not under the threat of raids then, so Merrow could afford to move her guerrieri out of the city to the Barrens. As I *hope* you know by now, Sera, six regiments are currently garrisoned here in the capital. We've already sent four to the western border with Desiderio. If we send another, we leave ourselves with only one."

"Yes, but—"

"What if the raiders who've been attacking our villages attack Cerulea instead and we have only one regiment of guerrieri left here to defend ourselves and the Matalis?"

"But we have your personal guard, too—the Janiçari," Serafina said, her voice—like her hopes of impressing her mother—growing fainter.

Isabella flapped a hand at her. "Another thousand soldiers at most. Not enough to mount an effective defense. Think, Serafina, think. Ruling is like playing chess. Danger comes from many directions, from a pawn as well as a queen. You must play the board, not the piece. You're only hours away from being declared heiress to the Miromaran throne. You *must* learn to think!"

"I *am* thinking! Gods, Mom! Why are you *always* so hard on me?" Serafina shouted.

"Because your enemies will be a thousand times harder!" Isabella shouted back.

Another painful silence fell between mother and daughter. It was broken by a frantic pounding.

"Enter!" Isabella barked.

The doors to Serafina's room swung open. A page, one of Vallerio's, swam inside. He bowed to both mermaids, then addressed Isabella. "My lord Vallerio sent me to fetch you to your staterooms, Your Grace."

"Why?"

"There are reports of a another raid."

Isabella's hands clenched into fists. "Tell your lord I'll be there momentarily."

The page bowed and left the room.

Serafina started toward her mother. "I'll go with you," she said.

Isabella shook her head. "Ready yourself for tonight," she said tersely. "It must go well. We desperately need this alliance with Matali. Now more than ever."

"Mom, please. . . ."

But it was too late. Isabella had already swum out of Sera's bedchamber.

She was gone.

TWO

TEARS THREATENED as the doors closed behind Isabella, but Serafina held them back.

Nearly every conversation with her mother ended in an awkward silence or heated words. She was used to it. But still, it hurt.

A slender tentacle brushed Sera's shoulder. Another curled around her neck. A third wound around her arm. Sylvestre, finely tuned to his mistress's every mood, had turned blue with worry. She leaned her head against his.

"I'm so nervous about the Dokimí, Sylvestre," she said. "My mother doesn't want to hear about it, but maybe Neela will. I've got to talk to *somebody*. What if Alítheia tears my head off? What if I mess up my songspell? What if Mahdi doesn't . . ."

Serafina couldn't bear to voice that last thought. It scared her even more than the ordeal that lay ahead.

"Serafina! Child, where *are* you? Your hairdresser is here!"

It was Tavia, her nurse, calling from her antechamber. Sylvestre shot off at the sound of her voice. There was no more time to fret. Sera had to go. She was expected—by Tavia, by the canta magus, by her entire court.

"Coming!" she called back.

She started toward the doors, then halte[...]
opened them, she was no longer Serafina. Sh[...]
or *Your Majesty*, or *Most Serene Principessa*. Sh[...]

She hated the hot-spring atmosphere of her [...]
the whispers, the glances, the toadying smiles. At co[...]
dress just so. Always swim gracefully. Never raise h[...]
Smile and nod and talk about the tides, when she'd much r[...]
be riding Clio or exploring the ruins of the reggia, Merrow[...]
ancient palace. She hated the suffocating weight of expectation,
the constant pressure to be perfect—and the pointed looks and
barbed comments when she was not.

"Two minutes," she whispered.

With a flick of her tail, she rushed to the opposite end of her
bedroom. She pushed open a pair of glass doors and swam onto
her balcony, startling two small sea robins resting on its rail.
Beyond the balcony was the royal city.

Cerulea, broad and sprawling, had grown through the
centuries from the first mer settlement into the center of mer
culture that it was today. Ancient and magnificent, it had been
built from blue quartz mined deep under the seabed. At this
time of day, the sun's rays penetrated the Devil's Tail, a protective thorn thicket that floated above it, and struck the rooftops,
making them sparkle.

The original palace had been built in the center of Cerulea.
Its roof had collapsed several centuries ago and a new palace
had been built high on a seamount—a baroque construction of
coral, quartz, and mother-of-pearl—for the royal family and its

The ruins of the reggia still lay preserved within the city,
a reminder of the past.

Serafina's eyes traveled over Cerulea's winding streets to the
spires of the Kolegio—with its black-robed professors and enormous Ostrokon, to the Golden Fathom—where tall town houses,
fashionable restaurants, and expensive shops were located. And
then farther still, out past the city walls to the Kolisseo, where
the royal flag of Miromara—a branch of red coral against a
white background, and that of Matali—a dragon rampant holding a silver-blue egg were flying. The Kolisseo was where, in just
a few hours, Sera would undergo her Dokimí in front of the
court, the Matali royals, the mer of Miromara . . .

. . . and Mahdi.

Two years had passed since she'd last seen him. She closed
her eyes now and pictured his face: his dark eyes, his shy smile,
his serious expression. When they were older, they would marry
each other. Tonight, they would be betrothed. It was a ridiculous custom, but Serafina was glad he'd be the one. She could
still hear the last words he'd spoken to her, right before he'd
returned to Matali.

"My choice," he'd whispered, taking her hand. "*Mine*. Not
theirs."

Serafina opened her eyes. Their green depths were clouded
with worry. She'd had private conchs from him when he first
returned home, carried by a trusted messenger. Every time one
arrived, she would rush to her room and hold the shell to her ear,
hungry for the sound of his voice. But after a year had passed,

the private conchs had stopped coming and official ones arrived instead. In them, Mahdi's voice sounded stilted and formal.

At about the same time, Serafina started to hear things about him. He'd become a party boy, some said. He stayed out shoaling until all hours. Swam with a fast crowd. Spent a fortune on mounts for caballabong, a game much like the goggs' polo. She wasn't sure she should believe the stories, but what if they were true? What if he'd changed?

"Serafina, you *must* come out now! Thalassa is due at any moment and you know she doesn't like to be kept waiting!" Tavia shouted.

"Coming, Tavia!" Serafina called, swimming back into her bedroom.

Serafina. . . .

"Great Goddess Neria, I *said* I'm coming!"

Daughter of Merrow, chosen one . . .

Serafina stopped dead. That wasn't Tavia's voice. It wasn't coming from the other side of the doors.

It was right behind her.

"Who's there?" she cried, whirling around.

The end begins, your time has come. . . .

"Giovanna, is that you? Donatella?"

But no one answered her. Because no one was there.

A sudden, darting movement to her left caught her eye. She gasped, then laughed with relief. It was only her looking glass. A vitrina was walking around inside it.

Her mirror was tall and very old. Worms had eaten holes

into its gilt frame and its glass was pocked with black spots. It had been salvaged from a terragogg shipwreck. Ghosts lived inside it—vitrina—souls of the beautiful, vain humans who'd spent too much time gazing into it. The mirror had captured them. Their bodies had withered and died, but their spirits lived on, trapped behind the glass forever.

A countess lived inside Serafina's mirror, as did a handsome young duke, three courtesans, an actor, and an archbishop. They often spoke to her. It was the countess whom she'd just seen moving about.

Serafina rapped on the frame. The countess lifted her voluminous skirts and ran to her, stopping only inches from the glass. She wore a tall, elaborately styled white wig. Her face was powdered, her lips rouged. She looked frightened.

"Someone is in here with us, Principessa," she whispered, looking over her shoulder. "Someone who doesn't belong."

They saw it at the same time—a figure in the distance, still and dark. Serafina had heard that mirrors were doorways in the water and that one could open them if one knew how. Only the most powerful mages could move through their liquid-silver world, though. Serafina didn't know anyone who ever had. Not even Thalassa. As she and the countess watched, the figure started moving toward them.

"That is no vitrina," the countess hissed. "If it got in, it can get out. Get away from the glass! *Hurry!*"

As the figure drew closer, Serfina saw that it was a river mermaid, her tail mottled in shades of brown and gray. She wore a cloak of black osprey feathers. Its collar, made of twining deer antlers, rose high at the back of her head. Her hair was gray, her eyes piercing. She was chanting.

The sands run out, our spell unwinds,
Inch by inch, our chant unbinds. . . .

Serafina knew the voice. She'd heard it in her nightmare. It belonged to the river witch, Baba Vrăja.

The countess had warned Serafina to move away, but she couldn't. It was as if she was frozen in place, her face only inches from the glass.

Vrăja beckoned to her. "Come, child," she said.

Serafina raised her hand slowly, as if in a trance. She was about to touch the mirror when Vrăja suddenly stopped chanting. She turned to look at something—something Serafina couldn't see. Her eyes filled with fear. "No!" she cried. Her body twisted, then shattered. A hundred eels writhed where she had been, then they dove into the liquid silver.

Seconds later, a terragogg walked into the frame, sending ripples through the silver. He was dressed in a black suit. His hair, so blond it was almost white, was cut close to his head. He stood sideways, gazing at the last of the eels as they disappeared. One was slower than the rest. The man snatched it up and bit into it. The creature writhed in agony. Its blood dripped down his chin. He swallowed the eel, then turned to face the glass.

Serafina's hands came to her mouth. The man's eyes were completely black. There was no iris, no white, just darkness.

He walked up to the glass and thrust a hand through it. Sera screamed. She swam backward, crashed into a chair, and fell to the floor. The man's arm emerged, then his shoulder. His head was pushing through when Tavia's voice piped up.

"Serafina! What's wrong?" she called through the doors. "I'm coming in!"

The man glared hatefully in her direction. A second later, he was gone.

"What happened, child? Are you all right?" Tavia asked.

Serafina, shaking, got up off the floor. "I—I saw something in the mirror. It frightened me and I fell," she said.

Tavia, who had the legs and torso of a blue crab, scuttled over to the mirror. Serafina could see that it was empty now. There was no river witch inside it. No terragogg in black. All she saw was her nurse's reflection.

"Pesky vitrina. You probably haven't been paying them enough attention. They get peevish if you don't fawn over them enough," Tavia said.

"But these were different. They were . . ."

Tavia turned to her. "Yes, child?"

A scary witch from a nightmare and a terragogg with freaky black eyes, she was about to say. Until she realized it sounded insane.

". . . um, *different.* I've never seen them before."

"That happens sometimes. Most vitrina are right in your face, but occasionally you come across a shy one," Tavia said. She rapped loudly on the glass. "You quiet down in there, you hear? Or I'll put this glass in a closet!" She pulled a sea-silk throw off a chair and draped it over the mirror. "That will scare them. Vitrina hate closets. There's no one in there to tell them how pretty they are."

Tavia righted the chair Serafina had knocked over, then chided her for taking so long to join her court.

"Your breakfast is here. So is the dressmaker. You *must* come along now!" she said.

Serafina cast a last glance at her mirror, questioning herself already. Vrăja wasn't real. She was of the Iele, and the Iele lived only in stories. And that hand coming through the glass? That was simply a trick of the light, a hallucination caused by lack of sleep and nerves over her Dokimí. Hadn't her mother said that nerves were her foe?

"Serafina, I am *not* calling you again!" Tavia scolded.

The princess lifted her head, swam through the doors to her antechamber, and joined her court.

THREE

"NO, NO, NO! Not the *ruby* hair combs, you tube worm, the *emerald* combs! Go get the right ones!" the hairdresser scolded. Her assistant scuttled off.

"I'm sorry, but you're *quite* mistaken. Etiquette demands that the Duchessa di Tsarno *precede* the Contessa di Cerulea to the Kolisseo." That was Lady Giovanna, chatelaine of the chamber, talking to Lady Ottavia, keeper of the wardrobe.

"These sea roses just arrived for the principessa from Principe Bastiaan. Where should I put them?" a maid asked.

A dozen voices could be heard, all talking at once. They spoke Mermish, the common language of the sea people.

Serafina tried to ignore the voices and concentrate on her songspell. "All those octave leaps," she whispered to herself. "Five high Cs, the trills and arpeggios. . . . Why did Merrow make it so *hard*?"

The songspell for the Dokimí had been composed specifically to test a future ruler's mastery of magic. It was cast entirely in canta mirus, or special song. Canta mirus was a demanding type of magic that called for a powerful voice and a great deal of ability. It required long hours of practice to master, and Serafina had worked tirelessly to excel at it. Mirus casters could bid light, wind, water, and sound. The best could embellish existing song-spells or create new ones.

Most mermaids of Serafina's age could only cast canta prax—or plainsong—spells. Prax was a practical magic that helped the mer survive. There were camouflage spells to fool predators. Echolocation spells to navigate dark waters. Spells to improve speed or darken an ink cloud. Prax spells were the first kind taught to mer children, and even those with little magical ability could cast them.

Serafina took a deep breath now and started to sing. She sang softly, so no one could hear her, watching herself in a deco-rative mica panel. She couldn't rehearse the entire spell—she'd destroy the room—but she could work on bits of it.

"Alítheia? You've never seen her? I've seen her twice now, my dear, and let me tell you, she's absolutely terrifying!"

That was the elderly Baronessa Agneta talking to young Lady Cosima. They were sitting in a corner. The gray-haired baronessa was wearing a gown in an alarming shade of purple. Cosima had on a blue tunic; a thick blond braid trailed down her back. Serafina faltered, unnerved by their talk.

"You have no reason to fear her, so don't," had always been Isabella's advice, but from what Sera had heard of Alítheia, that was easier said than done.

"The gods themselves made her. Bellogrim, the smith, forged her, and Neria breathed life into her," Agneta continued. Loudly, for she was quite deaf.

"Is there kissing during the Dokimí? I heard there's kissing," Cosima said, wrinkling her nose.

"A bit at the end. Close your eyes. That's what I do," the baronessa said, sipping her sargassa tea. The hot liquid—thick and sweet, like most mer drinks—sat heavily in an exquisite teacup. The cup had been salvaged, as had all of the palace porcelain, from terragogg shipwrecks. "The Dokimí has three parts, child—two tests and a vow."

"Why?"

"Why? *Quia Merrow decrevit!* That's Latin. It means—"

"'Because Merrow decreed it,'" Cosima said.

"Very good. *Dokimí* is Greek for trial, and a trial it is. Alítheia appears in the first test—the blooding—to ensure each principessa is a true daughter of the blood."

"Why?" Cosima asked.

"Quia Merrow decrevit," the Baronessa replied. She paused to put her cup down. "The second test is the casting. It consists of a diabolically difficult songspell. A strong ruler must have a strong voice, for, as you know, a mermaid's magic is *in* her voice."

"Why is that?" Cosima asked. "I've always wondered. Why can't we just wave a wand? It would be *sooo* much easier."

"Because the goddess Neria, who gave us our magic, knew that songspells carry better in water than wandspells. Danger is everywhere in the sea, child. Death swims on a fast fin."

"But why do we *sing* our spells, Baronessa? Why can't we just speak them?"

The baronessa sighed. "Do they actually *teach* you anything in school nowadays?" she asked. "We sing because song *enhances* magic. Why, song *is* magic! *Cantare.* More Latin. It means . . ."

". . . to sing."

"Yes. And from *cantare* come both *chant* and *enchantment*, *canto* and *incantation*, music and magic. Think of the sounds of the sea, child . . . whalesong, the cries of gulls, the whispering of the waves. They are so beautiful and so powerful that all the creatures in the world hear the magic in them, even the tone-deaf terragoggs."

The baronessa picked up a sea urchin from a plate, cracked its shell with her teeth, and slurped it down. "If, and only if, the principessa passes both tests," she said, "she will then undertake the last part of the Dokimí—the promising. This is where she makes her betrothal vows and promises her people that she will marry the merman chosen for her and give the realm a daughter of the blood, just as her mother did. And her grandmother. And so on, all the way back to Merrow."

"But *why*, Baronessa?" Cosima asked.

"Good gods! *Another* why? *Quia Merrow decrevit!* That's why!" the baronessa said impatiently.

"But what if Serafina doesn't *want* to marry and rule Miromara and give the realm a daughter? What if she wants to, like, open a café and sell bubble tea?"

"Don't be ridiculous. Of *course* she wants to rule Miromara. The things you come up with!"

Agneta reached for another urchin. Cosima frowned. And Serafina smiled ruefully. For as long as she could remember, she'd been asking the same questions, and had been given the same answer: *Quia Merrow decrevit.* Like many rules of the adult world, a lot of Merrow's inscrutable decrees made no sense to her. They still had to be followed, though, whether she liked it or not.

Of course she wants to rule Miromara! the baronessa had said. But the truth was, sometimes she didn't. She wondered, for a few rebellious seconds, what would happen if she refused to sing her songspell tonight and swam off to sell bubble tea instead?

Then Tavia arrived with her breakfast and started to chatter, and all such foolish thoughts disappeared.

"Here you are, my darling," she said, setting a silver tray down on a table. "Water apples, eel berries, pickled sponge . . . your favorites." She slapped a green tentacle away. "Sylvestre, keep out of it!"

"Thank you, Tavia," Serafina said, ignoring the tray. She wasn't hungry. She took a deep breath, preparing to practice her songspell again, but Tavia wasn't finished.

"I didn't get a chance to tell you this yet," she said, pressing a blue pincer to her chest, "but Empress Ahadi's personal maid was in the kitchens this morning, getting tea for her mistress. I happen to know that she's very fond of Corsican keel worms, so I made sure she got plenty. After her second bowl, she told me that the emperor is in good health and the empress is as bossy as ever."

"Did she?" Serafina asked lightly. She knew she must not betray too much eagerness for news of the Matalis, especially the crown prince. Her slightest reaction to any news of him would be noted and commented upon. "And the Princess Neela, how is she? When is she coming to my rooms? I'm dying to see her."

"I don't know, child, but Ahadi's maid—the one in the kitchens—she told me more things . . . things about the crown prince," Tavia said conspiratorially.

"Isn't that nice?" Serafina said. She knew that Tavia—a terrible gossip—desperately wanted her to ask what the *things about the crown prince* were, but she didn't. Instead, she practiced a trill.

Tavia waited as long as she possibly could, then the words burst out of her. "Oh, Serafina! Don't you want to know what *else* the maid said? She told me that the crown prince's scales are the *deepest* shade of blue, and he has an earring, and he wears his hair pulled back in a hippokamp's tail!"

"Mahdi has an *earring?*" Serafina exclaimed, forgetting for a moment that she wasn't supposed to be interested. "That's ridiculous. Next you'll tell me he's dyed his hair pink and pierced his tail fin. The last time I saw him he was skinny and goofy. A total goby, just like my brother. All he and Desiderio wanted to do was play Galleons and Gorgons."

"Principessa!" Tavia scolded. "Crown Prince Mahdi is heir to the Matali kingdom, and Principe Desiderio is a commander of this one, and neither would appreciate being called a *goby*! I should think you would at least be relieved to know that your future husband has grown into a handsome merman!"

Serafina shrugged. "I suppose so," she said.

"You *suppose* so?"

"It makes no difference if he's handsome or not," Serafina said. "The crown prince will be my husband even if he looks like a sea slug."

"Yes, but it's easier to fall in love with a good-looking mer-man than a sea slug!"

"Love has nothing to do with it, Tavia, and you know it. My marriage is a matter of state, not a matter of the heart. Royal alliances are made to strengthen bonds between realms and advance common interests."

"Fine words coming from one who's never actually *been* in love," Tavia sniffed. "You're your mother's daughter, that's for certain. Duty above all." She scuttled off to chide a chambermaid.

Serafina smiled, pleased she'd thrown Tavia off the scent. If she only knew.

But she didn't. And she wouldn't. Serafina had kept her secret, and she wasn't about to reveal it now.

She took a deep breath again and tried once more to practice her songspell.

"Coco, *stop* pestering Baronessa Agneta, and try on your gown!" a voice scolded. This time it was Lady Elettra, Cosima's older sister, who interrupted her.

"Gowns are *boring*," Cosima said, darting off.

And then Serafina heard another voice, secretive and hushed. "Is that what you're wearing to the procession? You shouldn't try so hard to outshine the princess."

There was laughter, throaty and low, and then a voice, beau-tiful and beguiling: "I don't *have* to try. It's no contest. He's only going through with the betrothal because he has to. Everyone knows that. He couldn't care less about it. Or her."

The words cut like shark's teeth. Serafina dropped a note and bungled the measure. She looked straight ahead, into the mica panel. In it she saw Lucia Volnero and Bianca di Remora, two of her ladies-in-waiting. They were at the far end of the chamber, holding up a spectacular gown and whispering. They didn't know it, but the room's vaulted ceiling channeled sound. Words spoken on one side of the chamber could be heard on the other, just as the ones speaking them could be seen in the mica panels.

Bianca continued the conversation. "What everyone knows, *mia amica*, is that you want him for yourself," she said. "Better give up *that* idea!"

"Why should I?" Lucia said. "A duchessa's daughter is a catch, too, don't you think? Especially *this* duchessa's daughter. *He* certainly seems to think so."

"What do you mean?"

"A clutch of us snuck out last night. We went to the Lagoon."

Serafina couldn't believe it. The Lagoon, the waters off the human city of Venice, was not far from Miromara, but it was forbidden to merfolk. It was a treacherous place—labyrinthine, dark, and full of dangerous creatures. It was also full of humans—the most dangerous creatures of all.

"You did *not*!" Bianca said.

"Oh, yes we did. It was totally riptide. We were shoaling all night. The Matalis, me, and a few other merls. It was *wild*," Lucia said.

"Did anything happen? With you and the prince?"

Lucia smiled wickedly. "Well, he *really* knows how to shoal. He has some fierce moves *and* . . ."

Bianca giggled. "And? And *what*?"

Lucia's reply was drowned out by a group of chattery maids bustling in with gowns.

Serafina's cheeks burned; she looked at the floor. She was hurt and furious. She wanted to tell Lucia that she'd heard every rotten word she'd said—but she didn't. She was royalty, and royalty did not shout. Royalty did not slap their tails. Royalty did not lose control. Ever. *Those who would command others must first command themselves,* her mother often told her. Usually when she complained about sitting next to a dull ambassador at a state dinner. Or got caught fencing in the Grand Hall with Desiderio.

She glanced at Lucia again. *She's always causing trouble. Why does she even have to be here?* she wondered, but she knew the answer: Lucia was a member of the Volnero—a noble family as old, and nearly as powerful, as her own. The Volnero duchessas had the right to be at court and their daughters had the hereditary privilege of waiting upon the realm's principessas.

Lucia, with her sapphire eyes, her silver scales, her night-blue hair swept up off her shoulders. You could bungle a hundred trills if you looked like that, and nobody would even notice, Serafina thought. Not that Lucia would bungle *anything.* Her voice was gorgeous. It was said the Volnero were descended from sirens.

Serafina didn't know if that was true, but she knew that Portia, Lucia's mother, had once enchanted Serafina's own uncle Vallerio. Portia and Vallerio had wished to marry, but Artemesia—the reigning regina and Vallerio and Isabella's mother—had forbidden the match. The Volnero had traitors in the branches of their family coral, and she hadn't wanted her son to marry into a tainted line.

Angry, Vallerio had left Cerulea and spent several years in Tsarno, a fortress town in western Miromara. Portia married someone else—Sejanus Adaro, Lucia's father. Some said she only married him because he looked like Vallerio with his handsome face, silver scales, and black hair. Sejanus died only a year after Lucia's birth. Vallerio never married, choosing to devote himself to the welfare of the realm instead.

Portia has taught Lucia her secrets, Serafina thought enviously. She sighed, thinking how *her* mother taught her the correct form of address for Atlantica's foreign secretary, or that Parliament must be convened only during a spring tide, never a neap tide. She wished that once, just *once*, her mother would teach her something merly—like which anemones to kiss to get those pouty, tentacle-stung lips, or how to make her tail fin sparkle.

Stop it, Serafina, she told herself. *Don't let Lucia get to you. Neela will know if Mahdi went to the Lagoon or not. Just practice your songspell.* She comforted herself with the knowledge that her best friend would be here soon. Just seeing her face would make this whole ordeal easier.

Serafina straightened her back, squared her shoulders, and tried, yet again, to practice her songspell.

"Your Grace, may I compliment you on your dress?" a voice drawled from behind her. "I hope you're wearing it tonight."

Serafina glanced in the mica. It was Lucia. She was smiling. Like a barracuda.

"No, I'm not, but thank you," she said warily. It wasn't like Lucia to be forthcoming with the compliments.

"What a pity. You should. It's so simple and fresh. Totally genius. Contrast is *absolutely* the way to go in a situation like this," Lucia said.

"Contrast?" Serafina said, puzzled. She turned to Lucia.

"Your look. It's a fabulous contrast."

Serafina looked down at her dress. It was a plain, light-blue sea-silk gown. Nothing special. She'd changed into it hastily, right after she'd swum into the antechamber.

"My look is all one color—blue. And we're in the *sea*, Lucia. So, it really doesn't contrast with anything."

"Ha! That is so funny, Your Grace! Good for you for joking about it. I'm glad it doesn't bother you. Don't let it. Merboys will be merboys and, anyway, I'm sure he's given her up by *now*."

The whole room had gone quiet. Everyone had stopped what she was doing to listen. Blood sport was the court's favorite game.

"Lucia, who's *he*? Who's *her*? What are you talking about?" Serafina asked, confused.

Lucia's eyes widened. She pressed a hand to her chest. "You don't *know*? I am *such* an idiot. I thought you knew. I mean, *everyone* knows. I—I'm sorry. It's nothing. I made a mistake." She started to swim off.

Lucia *never* admitted to making a mistake. Serafina saw a chance to best her, to pay her back for the mean things she'd said. And though a voice inside her told her not to, she took that chance.

"What mistake, Lucia?" she asked.

Lucia stopped. "Really, Your Grace," she said, looking deeply embarrassed. "I wouldn't like to say."

"No, tell me."

"If you insist," Lucia replied.

"I do."

As soon as the words left her lips, Serafina realized *she* was the one who'd made the mistake. Lucia turned around. Her barracuda smile was back. She'd only been feigning embarrassment.

"I was talking about the crown prince and his merlfriend," she said. "Well, his *latest* one."

"His . . . his *merlfriend*?" Serafina said. She could barely breathe.

"That's *enough*, Lucia! You're going too far!" Bianca hissed.

"But, Bianca, would you have me defy our principessa? She wishes me to speak," Lucia said. She fixed her glittering eyes on Serafina. "I'm *so* sorry to be the one to tell you. Especially on the day of your Dokimí. I was certain you knew, otherwise I would never have mentioned it. I only meant to compliment you by telling you that your look was a contrast to hers. All *she* has going for her is blond hair, turquoise scales, and more curves than a whirlpool."

Lucia, triumphant, dipped her head. Serafina felt humiliated, but was determined not to show it. This was her own fault. She'd stupidly fallen right into Lucia's trap and now she had to swim out.

"Lucia, thank you *so* much for telling me," she said, smiling. "It's *such* a relief to know. I hope she's taught him a few things."

"I beg your pardon, Your Grace?"

"Look, we all know it—it's no secret—the last time the crown prince visited, he was a bit of a goby and pretty hopeless with merls," Serafina said.

"You're not upset?"

"Not at all! Why would I be? I just hope she's done a good job with him. Taught him a few dance strokes or how to send a proper love conch. *Someone* has to. Merboys are like hippokamps, don't you think? No fun until they're broken in. Now, if you'll excuse me, I really do need to practice."

Lucia, thwarted, turned on her tail and swam away, and Serafina, a fake smile still on her face, resumed her songspell. The performance cost her dearly, but no one would have known. Used to the ways of her court, to its sharp teeth and claws, she was an expert at hiding her feelings.

Sylvestre, however, was not.

Crimson with anger, the octopus swam after Lucia. When he got close to her, he siphoned in as much water as he could hold, then shot a fat jet of it at her, hitting her squarely in the back of her head. Her updo collapsed.

Lucia stopped dead. Her hands went to her head. "My hair!" she screeched, whirling around.

"Sylvestre!" Serafina exclaimed, horrified. "Apologize!"

Sylvestre affected a contrite expression, then squirted Lucia again—in the face.

"You little sucker! I'll *gut* you!" she sputtered. "Avarus! After him!"

Lucia's pet scorpion fish zipped after the octopus. Sylvestre darted under the table where Serafina's breakfast tray was resting. Avarus followed him. The table went over; the tray went flying. Sylvestre grabbed a water apple and fired it at Avarus. Avarus ducked it and charged. He swam up to Sylvestre and stung him. Sylvestre howled, and a few seconds later, Serafina's antechamber was engulfed by a roiling cloud of black ink.

Serafina could see nothing, but she could hear her ladies coughing and shrieking. They were crashing into tables, chairs, and one another. When the cloud finally cleared, she saw Lucia and Bianca wiping ink off their faces. Giovanna was shaking it out of her hair. Tavia was threatening to hang Sylvestre up by his tentacles.

And then another voice, majestic and fearsome, was heard above the fray: "In olden days, royals had their unruly nobles beheaded. What a pity that custom fell out of use."

FOUR

THALASSA, the canta magus, was not amused.

She floated in the doorway of the antechamber, arms crossed over her considerable bosom, tentacles twining beneath her. Her hair, the gray of a hurricane sky, was styled in an elegant twist. A cluster of red anemones bloomed like roses at the nape of her neck. She wore a gown of crimson, and a long cape of black mussel shells. At a snap of her fingers, two cuttlefish removed it.

The entire chamber had gone quiet. Thalassa, Miromara's keeper of magic, was the most powerful songcaster in the realm. No one misbehaved in her presence—*ever*. Even Isabella sat up straighter when Thalassa entered the room.

"Causing trouble again, Lucia?" she finally said. "Nothing surprising from a Volnero. Do you remember what bad behavior got your ancestor Kalumnus? No? Let me remind you. It got him his head in a basket. Likewise your great-aunt Livilla. I would watch myself if I were you."

Lucia's eyes flashed menacingly at the unwelcome reminder of her ancestors' dark deeds. Kalumnus had tried to assassinate Merrow and rule in her stead. He'd been captured and beheaded, and his family banished. Two thousand years later, Livilla Volnero tried to raise an army against the Merrovingia. She, too, had been executed. Though these events had happened centuries ago, suspicion still shrouded the Volnero like sea mist.

"And *you*, Bianca," Thalassa continued. "A true di Remora. Always following the big fish. You might want to reassess your loyalties. The Merrovingia *are* Miromara and always will be. Alítheia ensures that." She waved a heavily jeweled hand. "Out. Now," she ordered. "All of you except the principessa."

Serafina knew that Thalassa had come to drill her on her songspell. She was her teacher.

"Your Dokimí's only a few hours away. As of yesterday, that trill in the fifth measure wasn't where it should be. It should be quick and bright, like dolphins jumping, not lumbering like a whale shark. We have work to do," Thalassa said.

"Yes, Magistra," Serafina said.

"From the beginning, please."

Serafina started to sing . . . and immediately stumbled.

"Again," the canta magus demanded. "No mistakes this time. The songspell is supposed to demonstrate excellence, and you are not even showing me competence!"

Serafina started over. This time, she got well into the songspell—and past the difficult trill—without a mistake. Her eyes darted from the wall ahead of her, where she'd focused her gaze, to Thalassa.

"Good, good, but stop biting off your words," Thalassa chided. "Legato, legato, legato!"

Serafina nodded to show she understood and tried to soften her words, gliding smoothly from phrase to phrase. She was doing more than merely singing now; she was songcasting.

Merrow's songspell, if sung correctly, told listeners of the origins of the merfolk. Like all principessas before her, Serafina had to cast the original songspell, then compose several movements of her own that illustrated the progression of the merfolk after Merrow's rule. She had to sing of her place in that progression, and her betrothed's, and she had to use color, light, and movement to do it. The greater her mastery of magic, the more dazzling her songspell.

She was just conjuring a likeness of Merrow when Thalassa started waving her hands.

"No, no, no! *Stop!*" she shouted.

"What is it? What's wrong?" Serafina asked.

"The images, they're far too pale. They have no life!"

"I—I don't understand, Magistra. I hit all the notes. I had that phrase totally under control."

"That's the problem, Serafina—too much control! That's *always* your problem. I want emotion and passion. I want the tempest, not the calm. Again!"

Serafina took a deep breath, then picked up where Thalassa had stopped her. As she sang, the canta magus whirled around her, pushing her, challenging her, never letting up. As Serafina began a very tricky section of the songspell, a tribute to her future husband, Thalassa swam closer, propelled by her strong tentacles.

"Expression, Serafina, more expression!" she demanded.

Serafina had conjured a water vortex as part of an effect. She added two more.

"Good, good! Now use the magic to make me *feel* something! Amaze me!"

Raising the vortices with her voice, Serafina made them taller and spun them faster. She forgot she was inside the palace, forgot to keep the magic small. Her voice grew louder, stronger. She swept a graceful hand out in front of her, curving the vortices. She bent them once, twice, three times, folding the water in on itself, forcing it to refract light.

"Excellent!" Thalassa shouted.

Sera's voice was soaring. It swooped over arpeggios, ranged up and down octaves effortlessly. She bent the water again and again, and a dozen more times until it cracked and broke into shards and light shot from it in so many directions, it looked like a mountain of diamonds glittering in the chamber. She was now coming to the part where she had to conjure an image of the crown prince.

She tried to make the most beautiful image she could imagine, but as soon as she saw Mahdi's face shimmering before her, her voice broke. All she could think about was Lucia telling her that he had a merlfriend. What if she was right?

All at once, her emotion boiled over. She lost control of her songspell. The vortices spun apart violently and splashed to the floor, knocking over a table, smashing a chair, and cracking two windows.

"I can't do it!" she shouted angrily, slapping the water with her tail. "It's an *impossible* songspell!" She turned to Thalassa, her composure entirely gone. "Tell my mother the Dokimí's off. Tell her I'm not good enough! Not good enough for her! Not good enough to cast this rotten songspell! And not good enough for the crown prince!"

FIVE

THALASSA PRESSED a hand to her chest. "What *is* this outburst?" she asked. "This isn't like you, child. You know the songspell inside and out. All you have to do is cast it!"

"Yes. Right. That's all," Serafina said hotly. "Just cast it. In front of the entire court. And the Matalis. And oh, I don't know, ten thousand Miromarans! It's too hard. I won't be able to pull it off. I'll bungle that trill. My voice isn't strong enough. It's not as *beautiful* as other voices are. It's not as beautiful as . . . as . . ."

Thalassa raised an eyebrow. "As Lucia's?"

Serafina nodded unhappily. To her surprise, Thalassa didn't lecture or scold. Instead, she laughed.

"Tell me, where does the voice come from?" she asked.

Serafina rolled her eyes. "From the throat. Obviously," she said.

"That's true for many," Thalassa said. "And it's certainly true for Lucia. But it's *not* true for you. Your voice comes from here." She touched the place over Serafina's heart. "It's a beautiful voice. I know. I've heard it. All you have to do is let it out. Show me your heart, Serafina. That's where the truest magic comes from."

Serafina laughed bitterly. "Show my heart? Here at court?

Why? So Lucia Volnero can stick a knife in it?"

"I heard what Lucia said. Ignore her. She wishes she were principessa. She wants the power, the palace, and the handsome crown prince," Thalassa said.

Worry darkened Serafina's eyes at the words *crown prince*. She blinked it away so quickly that anyone else would have missed it. But Thalassa was not anyone else.

"Ah," she said sagely. "So *that's* what's behind all this." She sat down on a settee and patted the place next to her. "Tell me, does he love you?"

"Yes. No. Oh, I don't *know*, Magistra!" Serafina said tearfully. "I think so. I *thought* so. But now I'm not sure. Not after what Lucia said." She sat down next to her teacher.

"Oh, Serafina," Thalassa said, putting an arm around her. "Have you told anyone how you feel? Your mother? Tavia? What do they say?"

Serafina shook her head. "I haven't told them. I haven't told *anyone*. I *won't*."

"Why not?"

"Because it'll get out somehow. The courtiers will find out and then it won't be mine anymore. It'll be theirs. You don't *understand*, Magistra. My whole life is public. I can't go anywhere alone. I can't do anything by myself. Every movement, every word, every look is talked about and picked apart. I wanted this, this *one* thing, for myself alone."

Thalassa took Serafina's hand. "You're wrong, you know. I *do* understand. I know something of a life lived in public. I *am* the canta magus, after all."

Serafina looked at her questioningly.

"My talent was recognized when I was a small child," Thalassa said. "A voice like mine, my teacher said, came along once in a millennia. I could fold water, throw light, and whirl wind by the time I was four. I was taken from my parents and given over to the Kolegio at six. By eight I was songcasting for your grandmother Artemesia and her court."

"How did *you* cope with it all, Magistra?" Serafina asked.

Thalassa laughed. "Poorly. When I was little, I took joy in my music. I cast my songspells simply because I loved to do so. But as I grew older and started songcasting for the court, I began to listen to what others said. I heard their remarks—some spiteful and cruel—and I believed them. I let their voices get inside of me, into my heart."

Thalassa released Serafina's hand. She touched her fingers to her chest, to the place over her heart, then pulled them away, wincing as they drew fine skeins of blood. The crimson swirled through the water like smoke in the air, then coalesced into images. As it did, Serafina saw the bloodsong—the memories that lived in her teacher's heart. She saw nobles from her grandmother's court whispering to each other behind their hands.

She'll never become a mage . . . Her voice isn't strong enough . . . It's too low . . . It's too high . . . Her trills are muddy . . . She's too fat . . . She's too thin . . . She's not pretty . . .

Thalassa waved the memories away. "I tried to please the voices. I started making music for them, not me, and my songspells suffered," she said. "Luckily, I saw what the voices were doing to me and I vowed never to let them in again. I guarded my heart fiercely. I closed it off. I allowed no one inside, nothing but my music."

"I'll do the same," Serafina said resolutely.

"No, child. I am telling you these things to convince you *not* to close your heart."

"But you just said—"

"What I *didn't* say, yet, is this: If you let no one into your heart, you keep out pain, yes, but also love. When I was sixteen, I wanted to be a canta magus. Music and magic were all that mattered to me. *You*, however, will become a ruler, and a ruler's greatest power comes from her heart—from the love she bears her subjects, and the love they bear her."

Serafina thought about Thalassa's words. She'd longed to share her feelings for Mahdi with someone. She'd longed to open her heart, but she'd been too afraid. Impulsively, she touched her fingers to her chest now and drew a bloodsong. She gasped as she did, for she was much younger than Thalassa and her memories were sharper. It hurt to pull them.

"I'm touched by your trust, child," Thalassa said. "Are you certain you wish to show this to me?"

Serafina nodded and Thalassa watched as the blood swirled through the water, taking on shape and color, making memory visible. Serafina watched too. It had happened two years ago, but for her it felt like yesterday. It had happened before the raids and disappearances. Before the tensions with Ondalina. Before the waters had grown so treacherous.

It had happened in the ruins of Merrow's ancient palace.

SIX

SERAFINA WAS HIDING.

From her mother, ministers, minions, and Mahdi.

She had stolen away. It drove everyone wild with worry, but she needed a few minutes a day, every day, to be free from the eyes and ears of the court. And she especially needed it today. The match had been decided. The announcement had been made. Serafina had met her future husband—and she didn't want any part of him.

Mahdi had arrived in Miromara a week earlier, with his parents, the emperor and empress; his cousins, Neela and Yazeed; and their royal entourage, to meet his future wife as custom demanded. He was sixteen—serious, smart, and shy. He didn't ride. He didn't fence. He preferred the company of Desiderio—Serafina's brother, a merboy his own age—and Yazeed to anyone else's. He barely spoke to Serafina, who was two years younger. He was courteous to her, as he was to everyone, but that was all.

"He's a goby. I'd rather marry Palomon," she told Tavia, referring to her mother's bad-tempered hippokamp.

Their first real conversation came about only by accident.

Serafina had been sitting in the gardens of the South Court, listening to a conch shell, when Mahdi and his chaperone, Ambassador Akmal, happened to swim by. They didn't see her. She'd hidden herself on a coral shelf above them, behind a giant sea fan.

"What do you think of the princess, Your Grace?" she heard the ambassador ask. "She is very lovely, no?"

Serafina knew she shouldn't be eavesdropping, but she couldn't help herself. Curious, she leaned against the sea fan.

"Does it matter what I think?" he'd said. "She's *their* choice— my parents', their advisers'—not mine. I have no choice."

At that very second, the sea fan—old and brittle—cracked under Serafina's weight. It fell from the coral shelf and toppled heavily to the seafloor, sending up a cloud of silt. When the cloud finally settled, Sera peered over the shelf. Mahdi looked up and saw her.

"Wow. This is awkward," she said.

"You heard us," he said.

"I didn't *mean* to," said Serafina. "I was sitting here listening to a conch and then you swam by and . . . well, I couldn't help it. Look, I'm sorry. I'll go."

"No, don't go. Please," Mahdi said. He turned to his ambassador. "Leave us," he ordered.

"Your Grace, is that wise? There will be talk."

"Leave us," Mahdi repeated through gritted teeth.

The ambassador bowed and left. As soon as he was gone, Mahdi swam up to Sera and helped her over the jagged edges of the broken sea fan. They sat down together on a nearby rock.

"I'm the one who's sorry," he said. "I shouldn't have said that."

"You don't need to apologize. I know how you feel."

He turned to look at her. "But I thought—"

Serafina laughed. "You thought what? That because I'm a merl, it's all just fine with me? Getting betrothed at sixteen and married at twenty? To someone chosen for me, not by me? How very enlightened of you, Your Grace. It's the forty-first century, you know, not the tenth. And to be perfectly honest, I'd much rather pursue a doctorate in ancient Atlantean history than marry you."

After that, she often felt Mahdi's eyes on her. They were beautiful eyes—dark, expressive, and fringed with long black lashes. She would look up at a dinner or during a pageant and catch him watching her. He would always look away.

The next time they were alone together, it was because Serafina had found *him* hiding. She'd had another history conch to listen to and had managed to sneak away from her court to do it. The only problem was that someone had beaten her to her new hiding place. Mahdi was sitting there, in a copse of kelp, with a knife in one hand and a small, ivory-colored object in the other. When he heard her approach, he tried to hide them.

"Can't you give me one moment's peace?" he'd asked wearily.

Serafina backed up. "I'm sorry. I didn't mean to disturb you," she said.

Mahdi's head snapped up at the sound of her voice. "Oh, *no*," he said. "*I'm* sorry, Serafina. I thought you were Akmal. He never leaves me alone."

"It's all right, Mahdi. I'll find somewhere else to—"

"No, wait, Serafina. *Please*." He opened his hand, showing her the object he'd tried to hide. It was a tiny octopus, about three inches long, intricately carved from a piece of bone.

"It looks just like Sylvestre!" she exclaimed, delighted.

"That was the idea," he said.

"It's *beautiful*, Mahdi!"

"Thank you," he said, smiling shyly. "Nobody knows I carve. I've managed to keep it a secret. I don't even know why I do it." He looked away. "It's just . . . sometimes you want one thing, just one thing—"

"—that's for yourself alone," she finished.

It was as if they were seeing each other for the first time.

"I have that with Clio," she said.

"Clio?"

"My hippokamp. I'm not allowed to ride by myself, being principessa and all. If I want to go out, I have to go with guards. But I always manage to get ahead of them and for a few moments, it's just Clio and me. All I hear is the sound of her fins beating the water. If a pod of dolphins swims by, I see it alone. If a whale passes by, I hear her song alone." She smiled ruefully. "Of course, if I fall off Clio and break my neck, I do that alone too."

When she finished speaking, Mahdi took her hand and placed the little octopus in her palm. "For you," he said.

A few nights later, she felt him take her hand again—this time in the dark, during a waterlights display in his honor. He'd looked at her, asking her with his dark eyes if it was all right. She'd answered him with hers that it was. And then, one evening while they were playing hide-and-seek with Desiderio, Neela, Yazeed, and the younger members of the court in the reggia, he'd suddenly pulled her deep into the tumbled ruins.

"I found you," he said, as they floated close together in the water.

"No, Mahdi, that's *not* how the game works. Don't you have hide-and-seek in Matali? It's not your turn. Desiderio's it," she'd said, keeping an eye out for her brother.

"I'm not talking about the game," he said. "I found *you*, Serafina. You're the one thing. The one thing for myself alone." He'd pulled her to him then and kissed her.

It was so lovely, that kiss. Slow and sweet. Serafina sighed as she relived it—then turned bright red when she remembered Thalassa was watching the bloodsong too.

There were more kisses in the days that followed. Stolen behind pillars. Or in the stables. There were long talks when they could break away, smiles and glances when they couldn't. And then, as Mahdi was leaving Miromara to return home, he'd given Serafina a ring. It wasn't gold or some priceless crown jewel taken from the Matalin vaults. It was a simple band with a heart in the middle, carved from a white shell. He'd made it for her, alone in his room at night. As he was saying his official good-byes in front of the court, he'd bent to kiss her hand. While he was holding it, he'd slipped the ring on her finger.

"My choice," he'd whispered to her. "*Mine.* Not theirs. I only hope that I'm yours, Serafina."

At that, the bloodsong spiraled into the water and faded away, and with it went the past.

Thalassa looked at Serafina. "And you *wonder* if he loves you, you silly merl?" she asked.

"I never used to, Magistra," Serafina said. She told Thalassa about the private conchs Mahdi had sent and how they'd suddenly stopped. "I've had only a few official communications over the last year. Nothing else. And now . . ." Her voice trailed off.

Thalassa cocked her head. "And now?" she prompted.

"And now he sounds like a very different merboy from the one I fell in love with. A riptide merboy with long hair and an earring, according to Tavia. And a merlfriend, according to Lucia," Serafina said unhappily.

"Lucia would say anything to upset you. You know that. She would love nothing more than to see you fail today, so you must triumph instead. Come, let's work on that trill again, and on the—"

They were interrupted by the sound of a door banging open.

"Serafeeeeeeeeeena!" a voice squealed.

Serafina spun around, startled. A mermaid floated in the doorway to the antechamber. She was wearing a yellow sari. Her glossy jet-black hair hung down to her tail fin. Her skin was glowing a pretty pale blue. She was flanked by servants, who were buckling under the weight of the gilded boxes, beribboned clamshells, and gossamer sacks they were carrying.

"Great Neria, who on earth—" Thalassa started to say.

But Serafina recognized the mermaid instantly. "Neeeeela!" she shouted, forgetting all her worries in the joy of seeing her best friend.

"Spongecake! There. You. *Are!*" Neela said. "I brought you sooooooo many presents!"

The two mermaids swam to each other and embraced, whirling around and around in the water, laughing. Neela was bright blue now. She was a bioluminescent, like a lantern fish or a bobtail squid. A bewitching light emanated from her skin when her emotions ran high, or when other bioluminescents were near.

"Princess Neela, you're *not* supposed to be here," Thalassa scolded. "We're right in the middle of songspell practice! How did you get in?"

"Tavia!" Neela said, grinning.

Thalassa frowned. "How many bags of bing-bangs did it take to bribe her *this* time?"

"Two," Neela replied. "Plus a box of zee-zees." She released Serafina, plucked a pretty pink box from a teetering pile, and swam to Thalassa. "I'm *so* sorry to interrupt, Magistra, really. May I offer *you* a zee-zee?" she asked, opening the box.

"You may not," Thalassa said sternly. "I know what you're up to. You can't bribe *me* with sweets."

"A chillawonda, then? How about a kanjaywoohoo? You *can't* say no to a kanjaywoohoo. And these are the very best. They take the palace chefs three full days to make. They have eight layers and five different enchantments," Neela said, popping one of the sweets into her mouth. "Mmm! Krill with a caramalgae filling . . . *sooo* good! See?"

"What I see is that our minds are elsewhere at the moment."

Thalassa sniffed, taking a sweet from the box. "You cannot stay long, you know, Princess Neela. Only a minute or two. We really *do* have to practice."

"Of course, Magistra. Only a minute or two," Neela said.

Thalassa, mollified, sampled the sweet. "Oh. Oh, *my*. Is that curried kelp?"

Neela nodded. She handed her another. "Beach plum with comb jellies and salted crab eggs. It's *invincible*."

Thalassa bit into it. "Oh, that *is* good," she said. "I suppose, perhaps half an hour's break might be in order," she said, her fingers hovering over the box.

Neela gave it to her. As Thalassa called to her cuttlefish servants to bring her a pot of tea, Neela grabbed Serafina's hand, pulling her out of the antechamber and into a wide hallway with windows on both sides, all of which were open to let in fresh water.

"Tail slap, merl!" she whispered, closing the doors behind them. "My evil plan succeeded. I thought you could use a break from practice."

"You thought right," Serafina said, grinning.

"Uh-oh. Opafago at twelve o'clock," Neela said.

It was no Opafago, but a palace guard swimming toward them.

"Your Grace? Is there something wrong? You shouldn't be in the hallways unescorted," the guard said.

Serafina groaned. Privacy, solitude, time alone with a friend. She dearly craved these things, but they were nearly impossible to find at the palace.

"Great whites at nine," Neela whispered, nodding at the group of maids advancing with mops and buckets.

"Good morning, Your Graces, good morning," the maids said, curtseying.

"A giant squid at six."

That was Tavia. "Serafina? Princess Neela? Why are you floating around in the hallway like common groupers?" She bustled toward them, glowering.

"We're surrounded, captain. I'm afraid there's only one way out of here," Neela said under her breath.

Serafina giggled. "You *cannot* be serious. We haven't done that since we were eight years old. And even then we got into trouble for it."

"I call Jacquotte Delahaye," Neela said.

"You *always* call Jacquotte!" Serafina protested. "She's the *best* pirate!"

"Don't be such a baby. You can be Sayyida al Hurra."

Neela swam to a window on the north side of the hallway. She narrowed her eyes at Serafina and said, "Abandon ship, chumbucket! Last one to the ruins is a landlubber!"

These were the exact words she'd said to Serafina when they were little, pretending to be pirate queens, and challenging each other to a race.

Serafina swam to a window on the south side. "Eat my wake, bilge rat!"

"One . . . two . . . *three*!" the mermaids shouted together.

A split second later, Serafina and Neela dove out the palace windows and were gone.

SEVEN

Determined to win the race, Neela swooped around a spire, then dove. Hurtling down through the water, she shot under an archway, startling the Matali dignitaries coming the opposite way, and made for the ruins of Merrow's reggia. She was swimming way too fast, but she didn't care. It felt wonderful to slice through the water, to feel powerful and free.

Serafina had zipped around a turret and under a bridge and was now gaining on her. Neela put on a burst of speed, but Serafina caught up. They touched the front wall of the old palace—as much of it as was still standing—at the same time, then collapsed on a pile of red coral weed, laughing and out of breath.

"Beat you!" Neela shouted.

"You did *not*! It was a tie," Serafina said.

"Yeah, except that I won."

"I can't believe we dove out of windows. We're in so much trouble."

Neela knew as well as Serafina did that swimming out of windows was bad form. Civilized mer came and went through doors. Aunt Ahadi would not be pleased.

"Yeah, we probably are, but it was worth it," she said, pulling two sweets from her pocket. "Here—purple sponge with pickled urchin. So good, you have no idea. Better than boys."

"That good?" Serafina said, taking the sweet.

"Mmm-hmm," Neela said, biting into hers. She was eating too many sweets. She did that when she was nervous. Like now. Sera was going to ask about him. That was a given. What on earth would she tell her?

Neela stretched out on the soft coral weed and stared up at the sun-dappled waters. "It's so good to finally be here," she said. "The trip was totally nerve-racking. The dragons we rode spooked at every guppy. The sea elephants carrying our trunks bolted twice. I couldn't sleep, because I was having bad dreams the whole time."

"Really? What kind of dreams?" Serafina asked.

"I can't even remember now," Neela said. She *did* remember, but she didn't want to talk about them. They were silly. "And Uncle Bilaal was *seriously* freaking out about Praedatori. He expected Kharkarias, their leader, to jump out at every turn. Even though he doesn't even know what Kharkarias looks like, since no one's ever seen him."

"You weren't attacked, were you?" Serafina asked.

"No, we were fine. We had lots of guards with us. But I was so glad to see the spires of Cerulea last night, I can't even tell you."

"I'm really happy you're here, Neela," Serafina said. "I can't imagine going through the Dokimí without you."

Sera hadn't asked about him yet. Good. Maybe she could

keep it that way. "How's the songspell? Are you nervous? What are you wearing?" Neela asked.

"Not great. Very. I don't know," Serafina said.

Neela sat up, startling some curious needlefish who'd come close. "You don't *know* what you're wearing? How can you not know? Hasn't the Dokimí been planned for years?"

"My dress is a gift from Miromara. The best craftsmer in the realm work on it. Only my mother sees it in advance. And anyway, it's not *about* the dress," Serafina said.

"It's *always* about the dress."

"I'm casting a songspell, not competing in a beauty contest. This is serious, you know."

"Merlfriend, *nothing* is more serious than a beauty contest. *Life* is beauty contest. At least that's what my mother always says," Neela said. "I can't wait for you to see what *I'm* wearing. It's totally invincible. It's a dark pink sari—the wrap is sea silk, but the top and skirt are made of thousands of tiny Anomia shells stitched onto tulle. I wanted it to be royal blue, but my aunt *insisted* on pink. I made it myself."

"You did *not*."

"I did. I swear it. But *shh*, don't tell anyone. You know how it is in Matali. Gods forbid a royal should actually *work* at anything," Neela said unhappily.

"Trouble with your parents?" Serafina asked, her eyes full of concern.

"That's an understatement. We fought about it for weeks. *Major* drama. I bet I ate twenty boxes of zee-zees. In one day."

Neela's dream was to become a designer, but her parents

wouldn't allow that. Or anything else. She was a Matalin princess and Matalin princesses were to dress well, look decorative, and one day marry—and that was all. Neela wanted so much more, though. Color made her heart beat faster. Fabric came alive in her hands. She had passion and talent and she wanted to use them.

Serafina took her hand. "I'm sorry, Neels."

"Oh, well. I can't ever be a designer, but I can pretend."

"You *are* a designer," Serafina said, suddenly fierce. "Designers design. That's what you did. And it doesn't matter who likes it and who doesn't."

Neela smiled. Sera was as loyal as a lionfish, quick to defend those she loved. It was one of the many reasons Neela adored her.

"I just hope Alítheia doesn't like pink. I don't want her thinking I look like a large and tasty zee-zee," said Neela. "Is it true she's ten feet tall?"

"Yes."

"Okay, like . . . *why?*"

"*Quia Merrow decrevit.*"

"Why the long, tortuous songspell?"

"*Quia Merrow decrevit.*"

"Why a betrothal at sixteen? That's totally dark ages. Wait . . . don't tell me. Let me guess."

"*Quia Merrow decrevit.*"

"But Merrow decreed it, like, *forty centuries ago*, Sera. The tides have come in and gone out a few times since then, you know?"

"I do. Believe me, Neela, I've listened to so many conchs

on Atlantis and Merrow for various courses, and I still haven't figured out why she made all her weird decrees. The whole Dokimí thing is barbaric and backward. It's from a time when life expectancy was short and principessas had to be ready to rule at a young age," Serafina said. "The weirdest thing is, this ceremony declares me an adult, fit to rule, and yet I have no more idea about how to rule Miromara than I have about flying to the moon. I can't even rule my own court." She sighed heavily.

"What? What's wrong?" Neela asked, her eyes searching Sera's.

"My court," Serafina said, making a face. "There's this one merl. . . . Her name's Lucia . . ."

"I remember her," Neela said. "The last time I was here, my skin had just started to glow. She told me I looked like fog light. In the nicest possible way, of course."

"That sounds like Lucia," Serafina said. "Neela, she said some things, about Mahdi."

Oh, no, Neela thought. *Time to change the subject.* "Hey, you know what? Let's swim," she said. "Why don't we head into the ruins? Stretch our tails? We can talk as we go."

Neela pulled Sera up from the coral weed and they set off, swimming, through what had once been a doorway. Time had crumbled its ancient arch. The walls of the old palace had tumbled down, and the roof along with them. Anemones, corals, and wrack had colonized the mosaic floors. In what had once been Merrow's Grand Hall, soaring blue quartz pillars still stood, hinting at lost glories.

"You should see the ruby necklace I'm wearing tonight. It's my mother's. It's completely invincible," Neela said as they swam together. She was babbling, desperate to keep the conversation from veering back to Mahdi.

"How are your parents?" Serafina asked.

"Great! Fabulous! They send their best and wish they could be here. But somebody has to hold down the fort in Uncle Bilaal's absence."

"And how are the emperor and empress? And your brother . . . and Mahdi?"

"Truly excellent. Although I haven't seen them yet today. We got in around eight last night. I was so tired, I went straight to my room and fell into bed. Everyone else did the same."

"Neela . . ."

"Oh! Did I tell you about the *last* state visit we all made? Ha! It's *such* a funny story!" Neela said. She launched into all the details.

Serafina wasn't really listening, though. "So, um, how's Mahdi?" she finally broke in.

Neela's heart sank. Her smile slipped.

Serafina stopped swimming. "What is it?" she asked.

"Nothing," Neela said brightly. "Mahdi's fine."

"He's *fine*? My great-aunt Berta is *fine*. What are you not telling me?"

Neela pulled another sweet from her pocket. "Oh, *super* yum. Candied flatworm with eelgrass honey. Try it!" she said.

"Neela!"

"Well, he's probably a *little* bit different from what you remember," she said. "I mean, the last time you saw him was two years ago. We're *all* different than we were then."

"Look, I know you're his cousin," Serafina said. "But you're also my friend. You *have* to tell me the truth."

Neela sighed. "All right, then—here it is: his royal Mahdiness seems to be going through a phase. At least, that's what Aunt Ahadi calls it. She blames it all on Yazeed."

"Your brother? What does he have to do with it?"

"Yaz is a total party boy. Always the one with the lampfish on his head. My parents are at their wits' end and Aunt Ahadi is *furious*. She says he's led Mahdi astray. The two of them are out *all* the time. It started about a year ago. That's when they got their ears pierced. Aunt Ahadi went through the roof. She and my mother threatened to beach them for life."

"That doesn't sound like the Mahdi I remember," Serafina said, nervously fiddling with some trim on her dress. "Neels, I have to ask you something else. Lucia said that—"

Neela unwrapped another sweet and bit into it. She made a face. "Yuck. Fermented sea urchin." She fed it to a passing damselfish.

"—she said that Mahdi has a merlfriend. She said he—" Serafina suddenly stopped speaking.

Neela, busy wiping her fingers on a frond of Caulerpa weed, looked up. That's when she saw them. Bodies. Of two young mermen. They were stretched out under a huge coral at the back of the courtyard, motionless.

Serafina panicked. "I—I can't tell if they're breathing or not. Neela, we have to get help. I think they're *dead*!" she said, swimming closer.

Neela panicked too, but for a totally different reason. "No, they're not dead," she said under her breath. "But if Aunt Ahadi hears about this, they're going to *wish* they were."

EIGHT

NEELA CAUGHT UP to Serafina and grabbed her arm. "Come on!" she said, trying to pull her away from the mermen. "This is dangerous. We should get the palace guards."

"But what if they're hurt or bleeding? We can't just leave them!"

"Yes, we can. We totally can."

Serafina broke free of Neela's grip and swam back to the bodies. "They're not dead! They're breathing and . . . *oh*. Wow. Didn't expect *that*."

Neela closed her eyes. She pinched the bridge of her nose. *How could they be so stupid?* she wondered. *How?*

"Um, Neela? It's *Mahdi* . . ."

". . . and Yazeed," Neela said.

She looked down at them. The two merboys were lying on their backs. Mahdi had a purple scarf tied around his head and smudged lipstick kisses on his cheek. A gold hoop dangled from one ear. His black hair was pulled back in a hippokamp's tail. Yaz was wearing a pair of sparkly earrings. Someone had drawn a smiley face on his chest with lipstick. He had a streak of pink in his cropped black hair, a heavy gold chain around his neck, and a tattoo on his arm. As she continued to stare at them, a large, homely humphead wrasse swam up to Yaz. It nudged his chin. Yaz flung an arm around it, pulled it close, and kissed it. As Mahdi snored on, Yazeed murmured compliments to the fish about her beautiful blond hair.

Neela, livid, gave each boy a hard slap with her tail.

"Ow!" Mahdi cried.

"Dang, merl!" Yaz yelped, letting go of the fish. "All I *said* was . . . *Neela?*" He blinked at his sister.

Mahdi, wincing at the light, said, "Yaz, you squid! Where *were* you? I was waiting for you. I decided to hang here until you caught up. I must've fallen asleep. Why are you *always* the slowest common denominator?"

"Yazeed, take those stupid earrings off! And sit *up*, both of you!" Neela scolded. "Serafina's here."

Mahdi paled. "What?" he said. "Oh, *no.*" He sat up. "Serafina? Is that you?"

"Nice to see you, too, Mahdi," Serafina said.

Her voice was cool, but Neela could see the confusion in her eyes. She'd hoped to keep her cousin's foolishness a secret from Sera. She'd hoped he could behave during his stay. Apparently, that was too much to ask.

"Look, Serafina, I need to explain," he started to say, getting up.

"Um, Mahdi? Are you *shimmering?*" Serafina asked.

"Hold on a minute . . . he's *shimmering?*" Neela said. She swam up to Mahdi and looked him over, and then Yazeed. Parts of them were shimmering, other parts were completely see-through. She grabbed her brother's gold chain and pulled it over his head. A small whelk shell dangled from it. As she turned it over, two pink pearls fell out.

"Transparensea pearls," she said. "Let me guess . . . you two cast pearls last night, then snuck out of the palace. When you tried to sneak back in, all the doors were locked. The windows, too. So you spent the night here, passed out under a coral. The only question is: Where did you go?"

"Nowhere," Yazeed said innocently. "Just out for a swim."

"Oh, please. I bet you went to the Lagoon. You did, didn't you?" said Neela, crossing her arms over her chest.

Yazeed looked around, suddenly interested in the architecture.

Neela glanced at Sera again. Her friend's eyes were on the lipstick kisses on Mahdi's cheek. They traveled to the scarf on his head. It had an L embroidered on it. *L for Lucia,* Neela thought. Her heart clenched as she saw the hurt on Sera's face.

"You're really something, Mahdi," she said angrily. "We are guests of the Merrovingia—invited here for your betrothal, I might add—and you go shoaling?"

"We weren't *shoaling*. We were, um, attending a concert. Broadening our cultural horizons," Yaz said.

Neela held up her hands. "Just. Stop," she said. She turned to her cousin, thumbed a smudge of lipstick off his cheek, and showed it to him. "Broadening your horizons?"

Mahdi had the good grace to blush.

"Neela," Serafina said in a small voice. "I have to get back."

But Neela didn't hear her. She was scolding her brother again.

As they continued to argue, Mahdi swam up to Serafina. "Hey, Sera . . ." he said haltingly.

"Sorry, Mahdi. I have to go," Serafina said.

"No, wait. Please. I'm sorry about this. Really. This is not how I thought we would meet again. I know how it looks, but things aren't what they seem," he said.

Serafina smiled ruefully. "I guess mermen aren't either."

Mahdi flinched at that. "Serafina," he said, "you don't know—"

"—*you,*" Serafina said. "I don't know you, Mahdi. Not anymore."

"Serafina!" Yaz shouted. "Help me *out,* merl! Tell Sue Nami here to cut me a break. All we did was hang out at the Corsair. The Dead Reckoners were playing. They're my favorite band. Mahdi's, too. We had to go. Otherwise, total FOMO."

"FOMO?" Serafina echoed.

"Fear of Missing Out," Yaz said.

"Don't encourage him, Sera. He thinks he's a badwrasse with his stupid gogg slang," Neela said.

"We started dancing and some silly merls recognized Mahdi and went crazy and drew all over us with lipstick. Then some swashbucklers told us there was an all-night wave going on in Cerulea, so we swam back," Yaz said. "That's all that happened. I swear!"

"An all-night wave in the ruins of the reggia?" Neela said. "Do you really expect us to believe that? It's a national monument!"

"Is *that* where we are? We're supposed to be in the Kolegio," Yaz said. He gave Mahdi a look. "Navigate much?"

Yaz was fibbing. Wildly. Neela was sure of it. He was trying to cover up whatever they'd really been doing.

"Look, I really do have to go," Serafina said. She was good at hiding her feelings, but this time even she couldn't pretend.

"Wait, Sera," Mahdi said, looking desperate. "I'm *sorry*. You're hurt, I know you are—"

"Oh, no. I'm perfectly fine, Your Grace," Serafina said, blinking back tears.

Mahdi shook his head. "*Your Grace?* Whoa, Sera, it's *me*."

"Yes it is. I guess Lucia was right," Sera said softly. She shook her head. "Don't worry about it, Mahdi. I'm fine. I *would* be hurt . . . if I cared."

NINE

"**G**OOD MORNING, Your Grace!"

"Good morning, Principessa!"

"All good things to you on this happy day, Your Highness!"

In the Grand Hall, courtiers bowed and smiled. Serafina thanked them, accepting their good wishes graciously, but all the while, her tears were threatening to spill over. Her heart was broken. She'd given it to Mahdi, and he'd shattered it. He was not who she thought he was. He was careless and cruel and she never wanted to see him again.

Sera was swimming fast to her mother's stateroom, where the business of the realm was conducted, to tell her what had happened. She knew her betrothal was a matter of state, but surely, in this day and age, no one would expect her to pledge herself to someone like Mahdi.

As she arrived at the stateroom, her mother's guards bowed and pulled the huge doors open for her. Three of the room's four walls were covered floor to ceiling in shimmering mother-of-pearl. Adorning them were tall pietra dura panels—ornately pieced insets of amber, quartz, lapis, and malachite depicting the realm's reginas. Twenty massive blown-glass chandeliers hung from the ceiling. Each was eight feet in diameter and contained thousands of tiny lava globes. At the far end, a single throne, fashioned in the shape of a sea fan and made of gold, towered on an amethyst dais. The wall behind it was covered in costly mirror glass.

The stateroom was empty, which meant Isabella was probably in her presence chamber, working. Serafina was glad of that. She might actually be able to have her mother to herself for five minutes.

The presence chamber was a much smaller room. Spare and utilitarian, it was furnished with a large desk, several chairs, and had shelves stuffed with conchs containing everything from petitions to minutes of Parliament. Only Isabella's family and her closest advisers were allowed inside it. As Serafina approached the door, she could see that it was slightly ajar. She was just about to rush in, sobs already rising in her throat, when the sound of voices stopped her.

Her mother *wasn't* alone. Sera peeked through the crack and saw her uncle Vallerio and a handful of high-ranking ministers. Conte Orsino, the minister of defense, was staring at a map on the wall. It showed Miromara, an empire that swept from the Straits of Gibraltar in the west, across the Mediterranean Sea, to the Black Sea in the East.

"I don't know if this has anything to do with the recent raids, Your Grace, but a trawler was sighted in the Venetian Gulf just this morning. One of Mfeme's," said Orsino. He looked haggard and bleary-eyed, as if he hadn't slept.

Vallerio, who was staring out of a window, his hands clasped behind his back, swore at the mention of the name *Mfeme*.

Serafina knew it; everyone in Miromara did. Rafe Iaoro Mfeme was a terragogg. He ran a fleet of fishing boats. Some were bottom trawlers—vessels that dragged huge heavy nets over the seafloor. They caught great quantities of fish and destroyed everything in their paths, including coral reefs that were hundreds of years old. Others were long-line vessels. They cast out lines fitted with hooks that ran through the water for miles. The lines killed more than fish. They hooked thousands of turtles, albatrosses, and seals. Mfeme didn't care. His crew hauled the lines in and tossed the drowned creatures overboard like garbage.

"I don't think the trawler has anything to do with the raids," Isabella said. "The raiders took every single soul in the villages, but left the buildings undamaged. Mfeme's nets would have destroyed the buildings, too." Her voice sounded strained. Her face looked troubled and tired.

"We've also had reports of Praedatori in the area of the raids," Orsino said.

"The Praedatori take valuables, not people. They're a small band of robbers. They don't have the numbers to raid entire villages," Isabella said dismissively.

Sera wondered how she knew that. The Praedatori were so shadowy, no one knew much about them.

"It's not Mfeme, either. He's a gogg. We have protective spells against his kind," Vallerio said. He'd left his place by the window and was swimming to and fro, barely containing his anger. "It's Ondalina. Kolfinn's the one behind the raids."

"You don't know that, Vallerio," Isabella said. "You have no proof."

Glances were traded between ministers. Serafina knew that her mother and uncle rarely agreed.

"Have you forgotten that Admiral Kolfinn has broken the permutavi?" Vallerio asked.

The permutavi was a pact between the two waters enacted after the War of Reykjanes Ridge. It decreed an exchange of the rulers' children. Isabella and Vallerio's younger brother, Ludovico, had been sent to Ondalina ten years ago in exchange for Kolfinn's sister, Sigurlin. Desiderio was supposed to have gone to Ondalina, and Astrid, Kolfinn's teenage daughter, was to have come to Miromara. Inexplicably, the admiral sent a messenger one week before the exchange was to have occurred to say that he was not sending her.

"In addition," Vallerio continued, "my informants tell me Kolfinn's spies have been spotted in the Lagoon."

"Kolfinn has not yet informed us why he broke the permutavi. There may be an explanation," Isabella said. "And Ondalinian spies in the Lagoon are nothing new. Every realm sends spies to the Lagoon. *We* send spies to the—"

Vallerio cut her off. "We must declare war and we must do it *now*. Before we are attacked. I've been saying this for weeks, Isabella."

Serafina shivered at her uncle's words.

Isabella leaned forward in her chair. "Desiderio sent a messenger with word that he's seen nothing—no armies, no artillery, not so much as a single Ondalinian soldier. I hesitate to declare war based on such flimsy accusations and without convening the Council of the Six."

Vallerio snorted. "You hesitate to declare war? You *hesitate*? Hesitate much longer, and the Council of Six will be a Council of Five!"

"I will *not* be pushed, Vallerio! *I* rule here. You would do well to remember that. I am not concerned with my life, but with the lives of my merfolk, many of which will be sacrificed if war breaks out!" Isabella shouted.

"*When* war breaks out!" Vallerio thundered back at her. He turned and smacked a large shell off a table in his anger. It shattered against a wall.

It was silent in the chamber. Isabella glared at Vallerio and Vallerio glared back.

Conte Bartolomeo, the oldest of Isabella's advisers, rose from his chair. He'd been refereeing these shouting matches since Isabella and Vallerio were children. "If I may ask, Your Grace," he said to Isabella, attempting to defuse the tension, "how are the preparations for the Dokimí progressing?"

"Very well," Isabella replied curtly.

"And the songspell? Has the principessa mastered it?"

"Serafina will not let Miromara down."

Bartolomeo smiled. "Is the principessa happy with the match? Is she in love with the crown prince? From what I understand, every female in Miromara is."

"Love comes in time," Isabella replied.

"For some. For others, it does not come at all," Vallerio said brusquely.

Isabella's face took on a rueful expression. "You should have married, brother. Years ago. You should have found yourself a wife."

"I would have, if the one I wanted hadn't been denied me. I hope Serafina finds happiness with the crown prince," he said.

"I hope so too," Isabella said. "And, more important, as a leader of her people."

"It's those very people you must think of *now*, Isabella. I beg you," Vallerio said. The urgency had returned to his voice.

Serafina bit her lip. Though they fought constantly, her mother prized his advice above everyone else's.

"What if I'm right about Ondalina?" he asked. "What if I'm right and you're wrong?"

"Then the gods have mercy on us," Isabella said. "Give me a few days, Vallerio. Please. We are a small realm, the smallest in all the waters. You know that. If we are to declare war, we must be sure of the Matalis."

"Are we not sure of them? The Dokimí is tonight. When Serafina and Mahdi are united, their realms will be united. Their vows cannot be broken."

"As I'm sure you recall, the betrothal negotiations with Bilaal were long and hard. I suspect Kolfinn may have been negotiating with him at the same time on behalf of his daughter," Isabella said. "The Elder of Qin, too, for his granddaughter. Who knows what *they* offered him. Their ambassadors are here at court to witness the ceremony. For all I know, they're *still* making offers. Until a thing is done, it is not done. I won't rest easy until Sera and Mahdi have exchanged their vows."

"And once they do, then you'll declare war?"

"Only if by so doing, I can avoid it. If we declare war on Ondalina by ourselves, Kolfinn won't so much as blink. If we do it with the Matalis' support, he'll turn tail."

Serafina remembered her mother's visit to her room earlier. Now it took on new meaning. *That's* why she'd been so worried about her songspell, and why'd she'd said they desperately needed an alliance with Matali. They needed it to avoid a war with Ondalina. Or to win one.

Moments ago, Serafina had been desperate to see her mother. Now she was desperate to slip away without being seen.

Isabella worked tirelessly on behalf of her subjects, always putting their welfare ahead of her own, always stoically bearing the burdens and heartaches that came with wearing the crown. Sera could only imagine what her mother would have said if she'd barged into her chamber complaining that Mahdi had hurt her feelings.

She had to do it. She had to put her pain and loss aside and exchange vows with a merman she couldn't even bear to look at, in order to save her people from a war. That's what her mother would do, and that's what she would do, too.

I always disappoint her, Serafina thought, *but tonight I won't. Tonight, I'll make her proud.*

TEN

"**Y**OU'RE TUBE WORMS. Both of you. No, actually, *tube worms* doesn't do you justice. *Lumpsuckers* would be better," Neela hissed. "Jackwrasses. Mollusks. Total guppies."

"*Shh!*" Empress Ahadi said. "Sit still and be quiet!"

Neela was quiet for all of two seconds, then she poked Mahdi in the back.

"You don't deserve her. She's way too good for you. I wouldn't be surprised if she's a no-show. *I* wouldn't get betrothed to you."

"I'll talk to her after the ceremony. I'll explain," Mahdi said.

Neela rolled her eyes. "'Hey, Mahdi, good idea!' said no one ever."

"Do I have to separate you like little children? The ceremony is about to start!" Empress Ahadi scolded.

Neela, Yazeed, Mahdi, and the rest of the Matalin royal party were seated in the royal enclosure inside the Kolisseo, a huge open-water stone theater that dated back to Merrow's time.

Isabella and Bilaal sat together in the front of the enclosure on two silver thrones. The regina was spectacular in a jeweled golden crown, her long black hair coiled at the nape of her neck.

A ceremonial breastplate made of blue abalone shells covered her torso and gossamer skirts of indigo sea silk billowed out below it. Emperor Bilaal was splendid in a yellow high-collared jacket and a fuchsia turban studded with pearls, emeralds, and—in the center—a ruby as big as a caballabong ball.

Serafina's father, Principe Consorte Bastiaan, and her uncle, Principe del Sangue Vallerio, sat directly behind Isabella. There was no re, or king, in Miromara. The regina was the highest authority. Males could be princes of the blood if they were sons of a regina, or prince consorts if they married one.

And in front of them all, on a stone dais, was a circlet of hammered gold embedded with pearls, emeralds, and red coral—Merrow's crown. It was ancient and precious, a hallowed symbol of the unbroken rule of the Merrovingia.

The empress and crown prince sat directly behind Bilaal. Neela and Yazeed were behind them. Fanning out from the royal enclosure were the Miromaran magi—Thalassa, the canta magus, the keeper of magic; Fossegrim, the liber magus, the keeper of knowledge—and the realm's powerful duchessas. Neela recognized Portia Volnero. She knew Sera's uncle had been in love with her once. She could see why: Portia, dressed in regal purple, with her long auburn hair worn loose and flowing, was stunning. Lucia Volnero was there too, drawing every eye in a shimmering gown of silver. Behind the duchessas sat the rest of the court—hundreds of nobles, ministers, and councillors, all in their costly robes of state. It was a sumptuous spectacle of power and wealth.

"Where's Sera?" Yazeed whispered.

"She's not in the Kolisseo yet. The Janiçari bring her here for the blooding, the first test," Neela replied.

She looked out over the amphitheater. Along its perimeter, the flags of Miromara and Matali fluttered in the night currents—Miromara's coral branch and Matali's dragon rampant, with its silver-blue egg. She knew the dragon depicted was a deadly razormouth, and that its egg was actually an ugly brown. The flag's designer, she guessed, had thought the egg too ugly and had changed it to silver-blue.

Every seat in the Kolisseo was taken and a tense, expectant energy filled the water. White lava illuminated the dark waters. It boiled and spat inside glass globes that had been set into large whelk shells and placed in wall mounts. To obtain the lava, magma was channeled from deep seams under the North Sea by goblin miners, the fractious Feuerkumpel, one of the Kobold tribes. It was refined and whitened, then poured into glass tough enough to withstand its lethal heat by goblin glassblowers, the equally unpleasant Höllebläser.

In the lava's glow, Neela could see the faces of the crowd. Many were excited. Others looked nervous, even fearful. *With good reason,* she thought. Generations of young mermaids had been crowned heiress to the Miromaran throne here, but others—imposters all—had died agonizing deaths. Her eyes flickered to the heavy iron grille that covered a cavernous opening in the floor of the Kolisseo. Twenty brawny mermen stood by it, wearing armor and holding shields. Fear's icy fingers squeezed her heart as tried to imagine what lurked underneath it.

Serafina must be terrified, she thought. *She's right—this is a barbaric ceremony.* It was hard to reconcile the Miromarans, a people so cultured and refined, with such a gruesome ritual.

"It's about to start!" Yazeed exclaimed. "I hear music! Look, Neela!"

He pointed to the archway on the opposite side of the Kolisseo. A hush fell over the crowd as a merman, grand and majestic, emerged from it. He moved at a stately pace, his red robes flowing behind him. A matching turban with a narwhal's tusk protruding from it graced his head. A scimitar, its gold hilt encrusted with jewels, hung from his belt.

Neela knew he was the Mehterbaşi, leader of the Janiçari, Isabella's personal guard. Fierce fighters from the waters off Turkey's southern coast, they wore breastplates made of blue crab shells and osprey-skull epaulets. A line of orca's teeth ran across the top of each of their bronze helmets.

The Janiçari followed their leader out of the archway, swimming in tight formation. Some played boru—long, thin trumpets. Others played the davul—bass drums made from giant clamshells. The rest sang of the bravery of their regina in deep, rumbling voices. It was an immense sound, intended to terrify Miromara's enemies. Neela thought it did the job well.

After twenty lines of Janiçari had marched into the Kolisseo, another figure—one very different from the fearsome soldiers— appeared in the archway.

"Oh, doesn't Sera look gorgeous!" Neela whispered.

"Merl's so hot, she melts my face off," Yazeed said.

"Wow. That's appropriate, Yaz," said Neela.

Mahdi stared silently.

Serafina sat sidesaddle atop a graceful gray hippokamp. She wore a simple gown of pale green sea silk. The color, worn by mer brides, symbolized her bond with her people, her future husband, and the sea. Over the gown, she wore an exquisite brocade mantle, the same deep green as her eyes. It was richly embroidered with copper thread and studded with red coral, pearls, and emeralds—the jewels of Merrow's crown. Her copper-brown hair floated around her shoulders. Her head was unadorned. Her face, with its high cheekbones, was elegant and fine. *But it's her eyes that make her truly beautiful,* Neela thought. They sparkled with intelligence and humor, darkened with doubt sometimes, and shone in their depths with love. No matter how hard she tried to hide it.

The second the Miromarans spotted her, they were out of their seats and cheering. The noise rolled over the amphitheater like a storm. Serafina, solemn as the occasion demanded, kept her eyes straight ahead.

The Mehterbaşi reached the base of the royal enclosure and stopped. His troops—with Serafina in the midst of them—followed suit. He struck his chest with his fist, then saluted his regina. It was a gesture of both love and respect. In perfect unison, all five hundred Janiçari did the same. Isabella struck her chest and saluted back, and another cheer went up. The boru players blew loud blasts.

Serafina's hippokamp didn't like the noise. She pawed at the water with her front hooves and thrashed her serpentine tail. Her eyes, yellow and slitted like a snake's, shifted nervously.

As Serafina calmed her, the Mehterbaşi turned to his troops and raised his scimitar, then sliced it through the water. As he did, the Janiçari moved forward, splitting their formation in the middle, so that half marched to the right, and half to the left. When they had ringed the amphitheater, the Mehterbaşi sheathed his scimitar, swam to Serafina, and helped her dismount. She removed her mantle and handed it to him. She would face Alítheia in only her dress. It would be her coronation gown or her shroud.

The Mehterbaşi handed her his scimitar, then led her hippokamp away. Serafina was alone in the center of the amphitheater. When the cheers died down she spoke, her voice ringing out over the ancient stones.

"Citizens of Miromara, esteemed guests, most gracious regina, I come before you tonight to declare myself of the blood, a daughter of Merrow, and heiress to the Miromaran throne."

Isabella, regal atop her throne, spoke next. "Beloved subjects, we the mer are a people born of destruction. In Atlantis's end was our beginning. For four thousand years we have endured. For four thousand years, the Merrovingia have ruled Miromara. We have kept you safe, worked tirelessly to see you prosper. Descended from the one who made us all, we are bound heart and soul, by oath and by blood, to carry on her rule. I give you my only daughter, this child of my body and of my heart, but I cannot give you your heiress. Only Alítheia can do this. What say you, good people?"

The Miromarans erupted into cheering again.

Isabella took a deep breath. Her back was straight. Her

manner calm. But Neela could see her hands shaking. "Release the anarachna!" she commanded.

"What's happening?" Yazeed whispered.

"This is the blooding, the first part of the Dokimí," Neela explained. "Where we find out if Serafina truly is a descendant of Merrow."

"What if she's not?" Yazeed asked.

"Don't *say* that, Yaz," Mahdi said. "Don't even think it."

Neela looked at him and saw that his hands were knotted into fists.

The armored mermen posted around the iron grille in the center of the amphitheater worked together to raise it. Heavy chains were attached to thick iron loops on its front edge. The mermen heaved at the chains and little by little, the grille lifted. Finally, it swung back on its hinges and clanged down loudly against the stone floor. A few seconds went by, then a few minutes. Nothing happened. The Miromarans, restless and tense, murmured among themselves. A few, very daring or very stupid, called the anarachna's name.

"Who are they calling?" Yazeed asked. "What's in the hole?"

Neela had studied up on the Dokimí ceremony. She leaned in close to him to tell him what she'd learned. "When Merrow was old and close to death," she explained, "she wanted to make sure only her descendants ruled Miromara. So she asked the goddess of the sea, Neria, and Bellogrim, the god of fire, to forge a creature of bronze."

"Duh, Neels. I know that much. I'm not dumb."

"That's highly debatable," Neela said. "When the

Feuerkumpel were smelting the ore for the creature, Neria brought the dying Merrow to their blast furnace. As soon as the molten metal was ready, she slashed Merrow's palm and held it over the vat so the creature would have the blood of Merrow in her veins and know it from imposters' blood. Neria waited until the bronze was cast and had cooled, and then she herself breathed life into Alítheia."

"Wow," Yazeed said.

"Yeah," Neela said. She looked at Mahdi. All the color had drained from his face. He seemed positively ill.

Yazeed noticed too. He leaned forward. "Mahdi, you squid! I *told* you to lay off the sand worms last night. They were way too spicy. Are you going to hurl? Want my turban?"

"I'm cool," Mahdi said.

But he didn't look cool. Not at all, Neela thought. His eyes were rooted on Sera. His hand was on the scimitar at his side. He was tense, as if he was ready to spring out of his seat at any second.

A roar—high, thin, and metallic—suddenly shook the amphitheater. It sounded like a ship's hull being torn apart on jagged rocks. An articulated leg, dagger-sharp at its tip, arched up out of the hole and pounded down against the stones. It was followed by another, and another. A head appeared. The creature hissed, baring curved, foot-long fangs. A gasp—part awe, part horror—rose from the crowd as it crawled all the way out of the hole.

"No. Possible. *Way*," Yazeed said. "M, are you seeing this? Because if you're not, then I'm, like, completely insane."

"Sera, *no*," Mahdi said.

Yazeed shook his head. "I can't *believe* that thing's Ala . . . Alo . . ."

"A-LEE-thee-a," Neela said. "Greek for—"

"Big, ugly, scary-wrasse monster sea spider," Yaz said.

"—*truth,*" Neela said.

The creature reared, clawing at the water with her front legs. A drop of amber venom fell from her fangs. Eight black eyes looked around the amphitheater—and came to rest upon her prey.

"Imposssster," she hissed.

At Serafina.

ELEVEN

QUIA MERROW DECRIVIT.

But how? Serafina wondered desperately. How could she have done this? How could she have forced all those who came after her to endure this?

Looking up at the massive creature, its bronze body blackened by time, Serafina was certain she would collapse from terror.

"You fear me! As you sssssshould. I will have your blood, imposssster. I will have your bonessss. . . ."

Alítheia scuttled toward her, her body low to the ground, her horrible black eyes glittering.

Serafina stifled a cry. In her head, she heard Tavia's voice, telling her the story of a treacherous contessa who'd lived hundreds of years ago. The contessa had stolen the real principessa when she was newly born, and put her own infant daughter— enchanted to look like the principessa—in her place. The young mermaid herself, the regina, and everyone else in Miromara believed she was the true principessa—everyone but Alítheia. She'd sunk her fangs into the mermaid's neck and dragged the poor imposter into her den. Her body was never recovered.

"We never know who we are, child, until we're tested," Tavia had said.

What if I'm not who I think I am? Serafina asked herself. She imagined Alítheia's fangs sinking into her own neck, and being dragged off, half alive, to the creature's den.

The spider skittered over the stones. She was only yards away now.

"No heiresssss are you. . . . Ussssssurper are you. . . . Death to all pretendersssss. . . ."

She circled, coming closer and closer, then lowered her head until her terrible fangs were only inches from Serafina's face. Another drop of venom fell on the stones.

"Who are you, imposssssster?"

Serafina felt her courage falter. She backed away from the creature, turning her eyes from its awful face. As she did, her gaze fell upon the mer seated in the amphitheater—thousands and thousands of them. She was their principessa, her mother's only daughter. If she failed them, if she swam away like a coward, who would lead them when her mother's time was done? Who would protect them as fiercely as Isabella had?

And suddenly she knew the answer to the creature's question. And the knowledge filled her with new courage and with strength. Bravely, Serafina faced the spider. "I am *theirs*, Alítheia," she said. "I am my people's. That's who I am."

She raised the scimitar the Mehterbaşi had given her and drew its blade across her palm. It bit into her flesh. Blood plumed from the wound. She raised her bleeding hand, palm up. The spider advanced.

"I am Serafina, daughter of Isabella, a princess of the blood. Declare me so."

Alítheia hissed. She pressed her bristly palps against the wound and tasted Serafina's blood. And then she reared up, screaming in rage. She spun away from Serafina and slammed her legs down, cracking the stones beneath her. "No flesshhhh for Alítheia! No bonesss for Alítheia!" she howled.

She scuttled around the amphitheater, menacing her keepers, trying to crawl over them and get at the Miromarans. The merpeople screamed and rushed from their seats, but the keepers held her back by brandishing lava globes. The white, molten rock, hot enough to melt bronze, was the only thing in the world the spider feared.

"Alítheia!" a voice called out loudly. It was Isabella. "Alítheia, hear me!"

The spider sullenly turned to her.

"What is your decree?"

Not a sound was heard. It was as if the sea itself was holding its breath. The spider crawled to the royal enclosure and took Merrow's crown in her fangs. She returned to Serafina and placed it upon her head. Then she bent her front legs in a bow, and said, "Hail, Sssssserafina, daughter of Merrow, princesssss of the blood, rightful heiressssss to the throne of Miromara."

Serafina made a deep curtsy to her mother. The cheer that went up was deafening. After a moment, she rose, carefully balancing Merrow's crown. It was heavier than she'd expected. Her heart was still hammering from her encounter with Alítheia, and her palm was throbbing, but she felt proud and exhilarated.

All around the amphitheater, the merfolk rose, still cheering. In the royal enclosure, Isabella and Bilaal rose, and the rest of the royal party followed their example. A bright flash of blue caught Serafina's eye.

It was Mahdi. He was wearing a turquoise silk jacket and a red turban. It killed her to admit it, but he was so handsome. She'd seen his face in her dreams for the last two years. It was different from what she'd remembered. Older. More angular. He caught her eye and smiled. It was beautiful, his smile. But it was a little bit awkward, too. A little bit goby. In that smile, Serafina saw the Mahdi she'd once known.

It made her heart ache to see that Mahdi. Where had he gone?

She didn't have long to dwell on that question, or the sadness it made her feel. The boru players blew a fanfare. The Mehterbaşi swam to her with her mantle and helped her back into it. Then he wrapped a bandage around her wounded hand.

The blooding was over. She knew what came next—the second of her tests, the casting. Her stomach squeezed with apprehension. This was the moment she'd worked so hard for, the moment when talent, study, and practice came together.

Or didn't.

TWELVE

NOW SERAFINA cleared her mind, of everyone and everything except for music and magic.

Magic depended on so many things—the depth of one's gift, experience, dedication, the position of the moon, the rhythm of the tides, the proximity of whales. It didn't settle until one was fully grown; Serafina knew that. But she needed it to be with her now, and she prayed to the gods that it would be.

Taking a deep breath, she pulled on everything strong and sure inside of her, and started to sing. Her voice was high and clear and carried beautifully through the water. She sang a simple, charming welcome to the Matalis, telling them how happy Miromara was to receive them. When she finished, she bent to the ground, scooped up a handful of silt, and threw it above her head. *Nihil ex nihil.* That was the first rule of sea magic: *Nothing comes from nothing.* Magic needed matter.

Serafina's voice caught the silt as it rose in the water, molded it, and then embellished it with color and light, until it took on the appearance of a lush island with bustling ports, palaces, and temples. She enlarged the image until it filled the amphitheater. Next, she summoned a shoal of small, silver fish. These she transformed into the island's inhabitants and as she did, her image became a living tableau.

The island, she told her listeners, was the ancient empire of Atlantis, nestled in the Aegean Sea. Its people were the ancestors of the mer. It was their story she sang now. Her voice was not the most beautiful in the realm, nor the most polished, but it was pure and true, and it held her listeners spellbound.

Using her magic, she showed how humans from all over the world: artists, scholars, doctors, scientists—the best and brightest of their day—had come to Atlantis. She showed farmers in their fields, sailors on their ships, merchants in their storehouses—all prosperous and peaceful. She sang of the island's powerful mages—the Six Who Ruled: Orfeo, Merrow, Navi, Pyrra, Sycorax, and Nyx. She sang of its glory and its might.

And then she sang of the catastrophe.

Heavy with emotion, her voice swooped into a minor key, telling how Atlantis was destroyed by a violent earthquake. Pulling light from above, pushing and bending water, conjuring images, she portrayed the island's destruction—the earth cracking apart, the lava pouring from its wounds, the shrieks of its people.

She sang of Merrow, and how she saved the Atlanteans by calling them into the water and beseeching Neria to help them. As the dying island sank beneath the waves, the goddess transformed its terrified people and gave them sea magic. They fought her at first, struggling to keep their heads above water, to breathe air, screaming as their legs knit together and their flesh sprouted fins. As the sea pulled them under, they tried to breathe water. It was agony. Some could do it. Others could not, and the waves carried their bodies away.

Serafina let the images of a ruined Atlantis fall through the water and fade. Then she tossed another handful of silt up, and conjured a new image—of Miromara.

Show them your heart, Thalassa had told her. She would. Miromara *was* her heart.

With joy, she sang of those who survived and how they made Merrow their ruler. She sang of Miromara and how it became the first realm of the merfolk. Her voice soared, gliding up octaves, hitting each note perfectly. She was conjuring images of the mer, showing them in all their beauty—some with the sleek, silver scales of a mackerel, some with the legs of crabs or the armored bodies of lobsters, others with the tails of sea horses or the tentacles of squids. She sang of Neria's gifts: canta mirus and canta prax.

She showed how the merfolk of Miromara spread out into all the waters of the world, salt and fresh. Some—longing for the places they'd left when still human to journey to Atlantis— returned to the shores of their native lands and founded new realms: Atlantica; Qin in the Pacific Ocean; the rivers, lakes, and ponds of the Freshwaters; Ondalina in the Arctic waters; and the Indian Ocean empire of Matali.

Then Serafina pulled rays of sun through the water, rolled them into a sphere, and tossed it onto the seafloor. When the sunsphere landed, it exploded upward into a golden blaze of light. As the glittering pieces of light descended, she depicted Matali, and told its history, showing it from its beginnings as a small outpost off the Seychelle Islands to an empire that encompassed the Indian Ocean, the Arabian Sea, and the Bay of Bengal.

She sang of the friendship between Miromara and Matali and conjured dazzling images of the emperor and empress, praising them for their just and enlightened rule. Then, though it pained her deeply, she showed herself and Mahdi, floating together in ceremonial robes, as they would be shortly to exchange their betrothal vows, and expressed her hope that they would rule both realms as wisely as their parents had, putting the happiness and well-being of their people above all else.

The images faded and fell, like the embers of fireworks in a night sky. Serafina remained still as they did, her chest rising and falling, and then she finished her songspell as she had begun it—with no images, no effects, just her voice asking the gods to ensure that the friendship between the two waters endured forever. Finally, she bent her head, as a sign of respect to all assembled, to the memory of Merrow, and to the sea itself—the endless, eternal deep blue.

It was so quiet as Serafina bowed that one could've heard a barnacle cough.

Too quiet, she thought, her heart sinking. *Oh, no. They hated it!*

She lifted her head, and as she did, a great, roiling sound rose. A joyous noise. Her people were cheering her, even more loudly than they had after the blooding. They'd abandoned all decorum and were tossing up their hats and helmets. Serafina looked for her mother. Isabella was applauding too. She was smiling. Her eyes were shining. There was no disappointment on her face, only pride.

She remembered her mother's words to her uncle in the presence chamber. *Serafina won't let Miromara down.* . . .

As the mer continued to cheer for her, Serafina's heart felt so full she thought it would burst. She felt as if she could float along, buoyed up by the love of her people, forever.

She would remember that moment for a long time, that golden, shining, moment. The moment before everything changed.

Before the arrow, sleek and black, came hurtling through the water and lodged in her mother's chest.

THIRTEEN

SERAFINA WAS FROZEN IN PLACE.

Her mother's chest was heaving; the arrow was moving with every breath she took. It had shattered her breastplate and pierced her left side. Isabella touched her fingers to the wound. They came away crimson. The sight of blood—on her mother's hand, dripping down her skirt—broke Serafina's trance.

"Mom!" she screamed, lurching toward her, but it was too late. Janiçari had already encircled her. They were shielding Serafina from harm, but also preventing her from getting to her mother. "Let me go!" she cried, trying to fight her way through them.

She heard the shouts of merpeople, felt bodies thrashing in the water. The spectators were in a frenzy of fear—swimming into one another, pushing and shoving. Children, separated from their parents, were screaming in terror. A little girl was knocked down. A boy was battered by a lashing tail.

Unable to break through the Janiçari, Serafina pressed her face between two of them and glimpsed her mother. Isabella was still staring down at the arrow in her side. The Janiçari were trying to surround her as they had Serafina, but she angrily ordered them to leave her and go to the Matalis. With a swift, merciless motion, she pulled the arrow out of her body and threw it down. Blood pulsed from her wound, but there was no fear on her face—only a terrible fury.

"Coward!" she shouted, her fierce voice rising above the cries of the crowd. "Show yourself!"

She swam above the royal enclosure, whirling in a circle, her eyes searching the Kolisseo for the sniper. "Come out, bottom-feeder! Finish your work! *Here* is my heart!" she cried, pounding her chest.

Serafina was frantic, expecting another arrow to come for her mother at any second.

"I am Isabella, ruler of Miromara! And I will *never* be frightened by sea scum who strike from the shadows!"

"Isabella, take cover!" someone shouted. Serafina knew that voice; it was her father's. She spotted him. He was looking straight up. *"No!"* he shouted.

He shot out of the royal enclosure, a coppery blur. A split second later, he was swimming up over the amphitheater— between his wife and the merman in black above her who was holding a loaded crossbow.

The assassin, barely visible in the darker waters, fired. The arrow buried itself in Bastiaan's chest. He was dead by the time his body hit the seafloor.

Serafina felt as if someone had just reached inside her and tore out her heart. "Dad!" she screamed. She clawed at the Janiçari, trying to get to her father, but they held her fast.

More Janiçari, led by Vallerio, surrounded Isabella. The Mehterbaşi had ordered another group to the royal enclosure, where they'd encircled the Matalis and the court.

"*Bakmak! Bakmak!*" the Mehterbaşi shouted. *Look up!*

Out of the night waters descended more mermen in black, hundreds of them, riding hippokamps and carrying crossbows. They fired on the royal enclosure and on the people. Janiçari raced through the water to fight them off, but they were no match for their crossbows.

"To the palace!" Vallerio shouted. "Get everyone inside! *Go!*"

Two guards took Serafina by her arms and swam her out of the Kolisseo at breakneck speed. Two more swam above them, shielding her. In only seconds, they were back inside the city walls and safely under the thicket of Devil's Tail. They continued on to the palace. When they reached the Regina's Courtyard, the guards broke formation and hurried her inside.

Conte Orsino, the minister of defense, was waiting for her. "This way, Principessa. Hurry," he said. "Your mother's been taken to her stateroom. Your uncle wants you there too. It's the centermost room of the palace and the most defensible."

"Sera!" a voice cried out. It was Neela. She'd just swum inside the palace. She was upset and glowing a deep, dark blue.

Sera threw her arms around her and buried her face in her shoulder. "Oh, Neela," she said, her voice breaking. "My father . . . he's *dead*! My mother . . ."

"I'm sorry, Principessa, but we must go. It's not safe here," Orsino said.

Neela took Serafina's hand. Orsino led the way.

As they swam, Serafina realized Neela was alone. "Where's Yazeed?" she asked.

Neela shook her head. "I don't know. He and Mahdi . . . they swam away. I'm not sure where they are."

They swam away? Sera thought, stunned. While her mother, bleeding and in pain, was daring her attacker to come forward? And her father was sacrificing his life?

"Bilaal and Ahadi? Are they safe?" she asked.

"I haven't seen them," Neela said. "Everything happened so fast."

The wide coral hallways of the palace, the long, narrow tunnels between floors—they had never seemed so endless to Serafina. She swam through them quickly as she could, dodging dazed and wounded courtiers. As she neared the stateroom, she heard screams coming from it.

"Mom!" she cried. Pushing her way savagely through the crowd, she streaked to the far end of the hall. A horrible sight greeted her there. Isabella lay on the floor by her throne, thrashing her tail wildly. Her eyes had rolled back in her head and red froth flecked her lips. She didn't recognize Vallerio, or her ladies, and was clawing at her doctor as he tried to stanch her bleeding. Serafina knelt by her mother, but her uncle pulled her away.

"You can't help her. Stay back. Let the doctor do his work," he said.

"Uncle Vallerio, what's wrong?" Serafina cried. "What's happening to her?"

Vallerio shook his head. "The arrow—"

"But she pulled it out! I don't understand . . ."

"It's too late, Sera," Vallerio said. "The arrow was poisoned."

FOURTEEN

SERAFINA WAS CRAZED WITH FEAR.

"No!" she shouted at her uncle. "You're wrong! You're *wrong*!"

Vallerio's tone softened. "Sera, the doctor's certain it's brillbane. He recognizes the symptoms. It only comes from one source—an arctic sculpin."

"An arctic sculpin," Serafina repeated woodenly. "That means—"

"—that Admiral Kolfinn has attacked us. The soldiers are wearing black uniforms—the color of Ondalina. They're Kolfinn's troops, I'm sure of it. This means war."

Serafina pushed him away, skirted around the doctor, who was pressing a fresh dressing over Isabella's wound, and sat down on the floor by her mother. She shrugged out of the costly mantle she was still wearing, balled it up, and put it under her mother's head.

"Mom? *Mom!* Can you hear me?" she said, taking her hand. It was covered in blood.

Isabella stopped writhing. It was as if Serafina's voice was a lifeline. She opened her eyes. Their gaze was far away. "Your songspell was so beautiful, Sera," she said. "I didn't get to tell you that."

"Shh, Mom, don't talk," Serafina said, but Isabella ignored her.

"Everyone looks so beautiful. The room does, too, with all the anemones in bloom and the chandeliers blazing and your father and brother, don't they look handsome?"

Serafina realized that her mother thought the Dokimí celebrations were taking place. The poison was affecting her mind.

"Why are you here, Sera? Why aren't you dancing with Mahdi?" Isabella asked, agitated. "Why don't I hear any music?"

"The musicians are taking a break, Mom," Sera fibbed, in an effort to soothe her. "They'll be back in a few minutes."

"He loves you."

Wow. She's totally out of her mind, Serafina thought.

"I glanced at him once or twice. In the Kolisseo. You should have seen his face while you were songcasting. I'm happy for you, Sera, and for Miromara. The bond between our realms will be even stronger if true love unites them." She grimaced suddenly. "My side . . . something's wrong."

"Lie still, Mom," said Serafina. "You have to rest now. How about we trade places for tonight? I'll be regina, you be principessa. And my first act as monarch is to order you to bed. You are to put your fins up, listen to gossip conchs, and eat plenty of kanjaywoohoos."

Isabella tried to smile. "Neela brought them?"

"And chillawondas, bing-bangs, janteeshaptas, and zee-zees. My chambers look like a Matali sweet shop."

Isabella laughed, but her laughter brought on a terrible fit of coughing. Blood sprayed from her lips. She moaned piteously. Her eyes closed.

"Help her! *Please!*" Serafina whispered to the doctor.

But the doctor shook his head. "There's very little I can do," he said quietly.

After a few seconds, Isabella opened her eyes again. Their gaze was not far away now, but focused and sharp. She squeezed Serafina's hand. "You are still so young, my darling. I haven't prepared you well enough. There's so much you still need to learn." There was an urgency to her voice.

"Mom, stop talking. You need to be still," Serafina said.

"No . . . no time," Isabella said, her chest hitching. "Listen to me . . . remember what I tell you. Conte Bartolomeo is the wisest of my ministers. Vallerio will be regent, of course, until you're eighteen, and Bartolomeo's the only one strong enough to put your uncle in his place." Isabella paused to catch her breath, then said, "Conte Orsino, I trust with my life. Keep a close eye on the Volnero and the di Remora. They are loyal now, but may work to undermine you if they sense an advantage elsewhere."

"Mom, stop!" Serafina said fearfully. "You're scaring me. I was only *joking* about being regina!"

"Sera, *listen* to me!" Isabella's voice was fading. Serafina had to lean close to hear her. "If we are not able to fend off the attackers, you must get to the vaults. And then, if you can, go to Tsarno. To the fortress there—" She coughed again. Serafina wiped the blood from her lips with the hem of her gown.

Vallerio joined them. The doctor looked at him. "Send for the canta magus," he said.

Serafina knew what that meant. The canta magus was summoned when a regina was dying, to sing the ancient chants that released a mer soul back to the sea. "No!" she cried. "She's going to be all right! Make her be all right!"

"Your Grace," the doctor said, his eyes still on Vallerio, "you must send for the canta magus *now*."

Vallerio started to speak, but Serafina didn't hear his words. They were drowned out by a deafening roar, a sound so big, it felt like the end of the world. The very foundations of the palace shook, sending shock waves up into the water. Serafina was knocked backward. For a few seconds, she couldn't right herself; then, slowly, her balance came back. She looked up, still dazed, just in time to see a large chunk of the stateroom's east wall come crashing down. Courtiers screamed as they rushed to get out of the way. Some didn't make it and were crushed by falling stones. Others were engulfed by flames ignited by lava pouring from broken heating pipes buried inside the walls.

Janiçari swam to the breach in formation, armed and moving fast. *"Ejderha! Ejderha!"* they shouted.

No, Serafina thought. *It's impossible.*

Grasping the side of her mother's throne, she pulled herself up.

And then she saw it.

Ejderha.

And she screamed.

FIFTEEN

A MASSIVE BLACKCLAW DRAGON, her head as big as an orca, stuck her face into the gaping hole she'd made in the wall. She reached an arm through, swiping at Janiçari with foot-long talons.

The soldiers attacked the beast, but their swords and their spells were useless against the thick scales covering her body, her bronze faceplate, and the stiff frill of spikes around her neck. Mermen wearing black uniforms and goggles sat on her back in an armored howdah, controlling her with a bridle and reins.

The dragon bashed her head against the palace wall and another large chunk of it fell in.

"Stop her! Stop her!" voices screamed.

But there was no stopping her. The stateroom was deep inside the palace. The dragon had already knocked through heavy outer walls to get here. An inner wall would be nothing to her. She would be inside the room in seconds.

"Get the regina to the vaults!" Serafina heard her uncle shout. "The princesses, too! Do it *now*!"

She knew he meant the treasury vaults underneath the palace, where the realm's gold was kept. The hallway that led to them was too narrow for a dragon, and the bronze doors enclosing them were a foot thick and heavily enchanted. Food and medical supplies had been stored within them in case of a siege.

Two Janiçari converged on Neela. Five more rushed to Isabella and tried to lift her. She screamed in pain and struggled against them.

"Mom, stop it. *Please*. You have to let them take you. You'll be safe there," Sera said.

Isabella shook her head. "Lift me onto my throne," she commanded her guard. "I will not die on the floor."

Serafina's heart lurched at her mother's words. "You're *not* dying. We just have to get you to the vaults. We just have to—"

Isabella took Serafina's face in her bloodied hands. "I'm staying here to face my attackers. *You* will go to the vaults, Sera. You are regina now, and you must not be taken. *Live*, my precious child. For me. For Miromara." She kissed Serafina's forehead then released her.

"No!" Serafina shrilled. "I won't go without you. I—"

She was cut off by a rumbling crash as the dragon knocked more of the wall down. The creature pulled her head out of the hole she'd made, and dozens of soldiers, all clad in black, swam inside. Their leader pointed toward the throne.

"There they are! Seize them!" he ordered.

Arrows came through the water. Many of the Janiçari surrounding the princesses and the regina fell.

"Go! *Now!*" Isabella shouted.

"I can't leave you!" Serafina sobbed.

Isabella's tortured eyes sought Neela's. *"Please . . ."* she said.

"What are we going to do?" Neela yelled. "I can't get them off me!"

"*Meu Deus!*" a new voice said. "I just *saw* him! He's with *her*!"

All three ghosts stopped short.

"What?" the first said.

"You saw him?" the second said.

"With *her*?" the third said.

A new mermaid—wearing glasses with round silver lenses, a lot of fuchsia, and holding a piranha on a leash—nodded gravely. Her skin was a warm chocolate brown. She had dozens of glossy black braids.

"I *did*. Swear to gods. He was *kissing* her. And they were laughing so hard. At you, *querida*. What's your name again?"

"Elisabeta!"

"Ileanna!"

"Caterina!"

"Oh, yeah. That's the name I heard him say. It was you, *mina*, for sure."

The three ghosts threw down the things they'd taken and screeched with rage. "Where *is* he?" they all shouted at once.

The mermaid pointed downriver. "That way. Just past the last village."

The ghosts raced off.

"*Tão louca!*" the mermaid said with a chuckle, watching them go. Then she said, "I'm Ava. *Tudo bem, gatinhas?*"

"Um . . . still alive . . . I think," Ling said. She turned to the others. "Ava just asked us how we are. In Portuguese."

"I'm not sure," Neela said, her hair hanging in her eyes. "What *was* that?"

"*Rusalka*, they're called. Here, at least," Ava said. "They're the ghosts of human girls who've jumped into a river and drowned themselves because of a broken heart."

"The Maiden's Leap!" Serafina said excitedly. "It's one of Vrăja's landmarks!"

"Maiden's Leap," Ava said, shaking her head. "*Maluca!* Must be something irresistible about rivers to sad girls. They just *have* to throw themselves into them. I've seen a lot of river ghosts. They're like vitrina, only mean. We have them in my river, the Amazon, but they have a different name."

"What do you call them?" Neela asked.

"Idiots!" Ava said, cracking up. "Can you imagine? Killing yourself over some guy?" She made a face. "*Ekah! Não faz sentido!* And I don't care how hot he is!"

The others laughed too. Serafina introduced herself, followed by Neela, then Ling.

"And you, *mina*?" Ava asked the red-haired mermaid.

"I'm Becca. From Atlantica," she replied. "Thanks for the backup."

Becca was kneeling on the riverbed, collecting her possessions and putting them neatly back in her traveling case.

"They gave you some nasty cuts. Your cheek's bleeding," Ling said. "I can't believe you were fighting them off by yourself."

Becca, smiling, shrugged off Ling's concern. "It's only a scratch," she said. "I've had worse."

"You're brave. You'd have fought them all day long," Ava said.

"If I had to," Becca said. Her eyes narrowed. "And *they'd* have come out the worse for it . . . eventually."

"One with spirit sure and strong," Ava said. "Felt that the second I met you, *mina.*"

Becca stopped repacking her things and looked at Ava. "How do you know those words?" she asked.

Ava was about to answer her, when there was a loud snapping sound.

"He tried to bite me!" Neela screeched. "I was only trying to pet him!"

"Careful," Ava said. "He has lots of teeth and no manners."

"What, exactly, are you doing with a piranha on a leash?" Neela asked huffily.

"He's my seeing-eye fish. I'd be lost without him. Wouldn't I, Baby?" Ava said, smiling at the growling piranha.

Baby stopped growling and smiled back.

"Wait, you're . . . you can't . . . I mean you're . . ." Neela stammered.

"Blind? Yeah. Totally. Can't see a thing." She lowered her glasses. Her eyes were pale and clouded.

"But you just saw us. You saw the ghosts," Serafina said.

"I *heard* you. And the ghosts. Felt you, too. My eyes don't work, but I still see. Just in a different way. I *feel* things. Sense them. Like a . . . *tubarão.* How you call it, *querida?*"

"Shark," Ling said.

"Like a shark. I felt the three of you days ago."

"You're the one Lena saw, aren't you?" Neela said. "She told us you'd crossed her patch of the river. . . . But you were ahead of us. How'd you get behind us?"

"I sensed you coming and I didn't know if that was good or bad. So I ducked out of sight. Let you pass. Felt you out. You"—she nodded in Serafina's direction—"are Merrow's daughter. I can tell by the way you got between those ghosts and your friends just now, like a warrior-princess. You"—she nodded at Neela—"you keep the light. I feel it coming from you, as warm as the sun. And you"—she nodded at Ling—"speak all creatures' tongues. Talk to Baby, will you? Tell him to behave himself."

Serafina and Neela looked at each other. *"One possessed of a prophet's sight,"* they said together.

"Becca makes four, and Ava makes five," Ling said. "Where's our sixth?"

"Let's ask the Iele," Becca suggested. "Maybe they can tell us."

"Maybe? Que diabo!" Ava said. "Witches *better* tell us where the sixth is, and a lot more, too. Think I came all the way over from Macapá to this cold, gloomy, *repulsivo* river to hear *maybe?*"

Becca snapped the lid of her traveling case closed. She rose and brushed the mud off her scales. "We should get going," she said briskly, pushing her glasses up on her nose. "Patrols could be near and we're still two leagues away, which—by my calculations—should put us there by evening *if* we swim at a moderate pace and don't encounter any more ghosts, strong currents, waterfalls, mermen in black uniforms, or—"

There was another snapping sound. And an indignant *"Hey!"* from Ling.

"Baby, what is *wrong* with you? Cut it out! She's a friend, not dinner!" Ava scolded.

Serafina and Neela traded glances. "I think we'd be safer with Traho, the death riders, and Rafe Mfeme all put together than we are with Baby," Neela whispered.

Serafina laughed. The others set off and she followed at a little bit of distance, watching Neela swim with Ling, and Ava with Becca. She'd taken an immediate liking to colorful, laughing Ava, and was intrigued by Becca, who seemed so organized and efficient.

Death riders were somewhere behind them, and the Iele were somewhere in front of them, and both scared her. But as she watched her oldest friend, and her three new ones, swim ahead of her, she felt surer and stronger about facing what was to come.

Neela turned around. "Sera, what was the next landmark again?" she asked, motioning for her to join them.

Sera swam to catch up, and the five mermaids continued up the Olt. Together.

THIRTY-SEVEN

T HE RIVER GREW murkier and colder, the farther the mermaids swam up it.

"We're close now," Serafina said, as they put the last two leagues behind them. "We have to be. *Two leagues past the Maiden's Leap*—that's what Vrăja said. *In the waters of the Malacostraca.*"

"What's a Malacostraca?" Neela asked.

"I have no idea."

Serafina looked around anxiously for any sign of a cave, a doorway—anything that might lead to the Iele. The sun was starting to set. Looking up through the water, Serafina saw a flock of crows pass overhead. Their dark silhouettes seemed ominous to her. She returned her gaze to the waters in front of her, sweeping her eyes left to right, alert for danger. There were hollows in the river's banks. Creatures darted in and out of them. She felt them watching as she passed and hoped there were no more rotters lurking.

"We're getting closer every minute, aren't we?" Neela said. "Please say we are. This river gives me the creeps."

"We better be," Ava said. "I feel something now. Coming up behind us. Coming up fast."

"Great," Ling said, looking over her shoulder.

"By my calculations, the cave should be right here," Becca said, glancing around.

"As much as I want to get there," Neela said, "I don't want to get there."

"I know what you mean," Becca said. "I just can't believe this. I traveled thousands of miles, on the spur of the moment, all because of a dream. I don't do things like this. *Ever.* I told my parents I was checking out a college in the Dunărea. How could I tell them the truth? 'Mom, Dad . . . I'm going to visit some witches. I don't know for sure where they live, or if they actually exist, or what I'm supposed to do once I find them. But hey, I just have to do it. Don't ask me why.' I had to take time off my after-school job as well."

"Where do you work, *mina*?" Ava asked.

"In a songpearl shop. As a spellbinder. I take ready-made spells, then heat pearls—Caribbean pinks—in a lava forge until they expand, and insert the spells. We export the pearls all over the world. The shop's called Baudel's."

"Baudel's?" Neela squealed. "I know Baudel's! I *love* their stuff. My family orders *tons* of their songpearls—decorating spells, party spells, hairstyling spells, makeup spells. What's coming out for the new season?"

Serafina could hear the worry in their voices under the chattery excitement. They were talking about anything—anything at all—to take their minds off their fears. The goggs had a good expression for it: whistling in the dark.

"Well," Becca said, "I'm *really* excited about the new Whirlpearl Glitterbomb. It's part of our Cast-to-Last line."

"I love it!" Neela said. "What is it?"

"We take a pink pearl and we pack it with glitter spells in ten different colorways. When you cast it, your hair, eyelids, lips, and fins will sparkle silver, blue, green—whatever you choose—for two weeks. No dulling, no fading. Guaranteed." She smiled shyly, then added, "It was my idea. The first one I ever pitched."

Neela pressed a hand to her chest. "Darling, *when* can I get them?"

"Um, merls?" Ling said, stopping short.

"They're coming out this winter," Becca said.

"Do they come in fuchsia, *mina*?" Ava asked. "Everyone tells me that's my color."

"Ladies? *Hel-lo!*" Ling said. "I think we've arrived."

She pointed ahead—at the biggest crayfish any of them had ever seen. The chatter stopped. There were two of them. They were dark brown with shiny black eyes, and powerfully built. As the mermaids watched, they rose up and pressed their claws against a large rock. It rolled a few feet through the river mud, revealing a passageway. A freshwater mermaid, her body stippled in a hundred shades of brown and gray, swam out of it. Her face was pale; her hair was dark and flowing. She wore a necklace of fox teeth and a fitted gown of gray herons. Snake skeletons twined around each arm.

Serafina recognized her. She was one of the witches who'd chanted in her dream. One of the Iele. At last.

They'd made it. With the help of the others. They were finally here. Soon they would learn why they had been summoned.

The witch spoke briefly with the crayfish. Their bristly mandibles opened and closed rapidly. Their long antennae waved. The witch nodded, then turned to the mermaids.

"I am Magdalena, of the Iele. The Malacostraca tell me that they sense enemies half a league south and moving fast," she said. "This way, please. Hurry."

Serafina, Ava, Ling, and Becca swam inside. Neela followed them, but at the very last second, shied. "I can't," she said. "Once I go in, there's no way out again. This is real. *You're* real. All this time, a part of me was hoping you were only a dream."

The witch cocked her head. "*Only* a dream?" she said mockingly. "Long ago, a great mage dreamed of stealing the gods' powers. Abbadon was born of that dream. Atlantis died because of it. Now, because of a new dreamer, all the waters of the world may fall. There is *nothing* more real than a dream." She nodded at the waters behind Neela. Silt was rising in the distance, a great deal of it. "The merman Traho knows this. He's coming. If you do not believe me, perhaps he can convince you."

Neela, paralyzed by fear, stayed where she was, eyes squeezed shut. The sound of beating fins was growing louder. The death riders were closing in.

Serafina pushed past the witch and swam back out of the tunnel. She took Neela's hand. "We go in together, Neels," she said. "Together, or not at all."

Ava joined them. "Together," she said, placing her hand over Neela's and Sera's. Ling and Becca did the same.

Neela opened her eyes and Sera saw that the fear was gone. It had been replaced by something else: faith. Faith in her. Faith in the others. Faith in the bond between them, however new and fragile.

"Together," Neela said.

She swam into the tunnel. The others followed. As soon as they were all inside, the Malacostraca moved the rock back into place and used their tail fins to sweep away the tracks it had made in the mud. When they finished, the creatures hid themselves—one under a submerged tree trunk, one under a blanket of rotting leaves.

Half a minute later, Traho and fifty death riders thundered by.

THIRTY-EIGHT

As THE MALACOSTRACA rolled the heavy stone back across the entrance to the Iele's caves, blocking off the light from above, Serafina felt like she was being sealed inside a tomb.

"I will take you to the obârşie now, our leader," Magdalena said.

She led them down a murky passageway. It was lit by sputtering lava globes and spiraled downward, branching into a network of tunnels carved into the rock by the river. As her eyes adjusted to the gloomy waters, Serafina saw that many guards—tall, golden-eyed frogs—flanked the passageway. They held long, steel-tipped spears at an angle from their bodies, creating an X between them. As the witch approached, they snapped their spears back smartly, allowing her to pass. Serafina and the others hurried along behind her. It was quiet in the passageway.

"No one will be able to get in, at least. Not with that giant rock blocking the entrance," Becca whispered. "That's a comfort."

"And no one will be able to get out," Ling said. "That's not."

"Anyone have a spare zee-zee?" Neela asked in a shaky voice.

No one answered her, and the witch led them farther down the passage. Just as it seemed she would lead them straight to the center of the earth, she stopped in front of a wooden door heavily carved with runes. A fierce-looking sturgeon, his back knobby and spiked, his barbels so long they touched the floor, pulled it open. Magdalena led them inside.

Serafina looked around. The room appeared to be some-one's study. A huge stone desk, its top intricately inset with onyx, stood at the far end. Behind it was a tall chair made of antlers and bones. More chairs, all made of driftwood, were scattered about. Shelves hewn out of the rock held animal skulls, fresh-water shells, and stone jars with odd creatures half in and half out of them, blinking and slithering. Plump black leeches inched up the walls. A spotted salamander skittered across the ceiling. Becca put down her traveling case. Neela dropped her messenger bag on the floor.

"Wait here. Baba Vrăja will see you shortly," Magdalena said. She swam out of the room and the sturgeon closed the doors behind her. The mermaids were alone.

Or so they thought.

The room was filled with so many curious things that it took a few seconds for Serafina to see that there was another mermaid in it. Her back was to them. She wore a long sealskin vest embroidered with silver thread. A scabbard made from eel-skin hung from her waist. Her tail had the bold black and white markings of an orca. Two ornate braids ran along the sides of her head; the rest of her white-blond hair flowed long and loose.

She turned suddenly, and Serafina gasped as she looked into a pair of icy blue eyes.

It was Astrid.

Admiral Kolfinn's daughter.

From Ondalina.

THIRTY-NINE

SERAFINA'S TAIL thrashed furiously. Alarms went off in her head.

It's a trap! she thought. *How could I have been so stupid?*

"Coward!" she snarled at Astrid. "Ambushing us like this! Did you come alone? Or did you bring your assassins?"

"You!" Astrid spat. "This is typical Merrovingian treachery. Good thing you brought backup, Principessa. You'll need it!"

Astrid lunged, fins flaring. Serafina dodged her. The two whirled around a chair, poised to attack. Baby went wild. Ava could barely contain him.

"Merls, hey . . . that's *enough*," Ling warned, but Sera and Astrid ignored her.

Serafina's fury was alive. She could feel it, roiling and twisting inside her, wrapping its red tentacles around her heart. She could hear its laughter—gurgling and low.

"First your spies try to kill my father by putting a sea burr under his saddle—one that only grows in Miromaran waters," Astrid hissed. "You'll be disappointed to know he only broke some ribs, not his neck. Then they mixed poison into his supper. Venom from a Medusa anemone. You know those, don't you, Sera*fienda? They* grow in the reefs off Cerulea!"

"Don't accuse Miromara of using Ondalina's methods! The assassin's arrow that wounded my mother was dipped in brill-bane. Cerulea was attacked by soldiers wearing the uniforms of Ondalina. I was there. I *saw* them!"

"Stop, both of you! *Please!*" Neela begged.

"Your father's soldiers destroyed my city!" Serafina shouted. She swept a handful of water into a ball and hurled it at Astrid, casting a stilo songspell as she did. Spikes sprouted from the ball as it neared its target.

"Isabella ordered my father's death!" Astrid yelled, deftly ducking the missile. She did not fire back with a spell of her own. Instead, she pulled her sword from its scabbard, and swung it at Serafina.

"Kolfinn killed hundreds of innocent people!" Serafina spat, parrying the blade with a deflecto spell. It crashed down across the water shield she'd conjured, spraying droplets like shrapnel.

A door located behind the stone desk suddenly banged back on its hinges. An elderly mermaid swam through it. She was dressed in a long black cloak, a ruff of ebony swan feathers at her neck. Her gray hair was coiled at the back of her head. On her hands she wore rings carved from amber. Their prongs held eyeballs that swiveled and stared. Her own eyes blazed with anger.

"You *fools*! How *dare* you behave this way in the presence of the Iele!" she thundered.

Serafina and Astrid stopped still, the red trance of rage broken.

"You were not summoned here to fight. That's exactly what the monster wants. It wants you to destroy each other."

"You're Baba Vrăja, aren't you?" Neela said, her eyes wide, her voice hushed with awe. "Oh. My. *Gods*. I can't believe it. I saw you in my dream. But Duca Armando said the Iele are only myths, like the ones ancients told to explain thunderstorms. He said you were just a story."

"Then your duca's a fool," said the witch. "Stories don't tell us what a thunderstorm is, they tell us what *we* are." She looked each of the six mermaids over in turn, her black eyes glittering. "Come. Follow me and I will show you an adversary worth fighting."

Before anyone could respond, Vrăja turned and swam back through the doorway. Neela, Ling, Serafina, and Becca were right behind her. Ava warned Baby to stay put, then followed the others. Astrid brought up the rear. Vrăja led them down a winding tunnel. They had to move fast to keep up with her. Some young river witches were swimming up the tunnel in the opposite direction. They touched their steepled hands to their foreheads as they approached her. One was bruised. Another bloodied. One, nearly unconscious, was being carried.

"Tell me again why we came here?" Neela whispered nervously.

"I think we're about to find out," Serafina said.

"I hear chanting," Becca said.

"Me too," Ling said. "Ava, can you see anything?"

"Not so much as a minnow," Ava replied. "Is there iron nearby?"

"Yes. An iron door. Up ahead of us," Ling said.

"Where does this crazy little tour end, anyway?" Astrid called out from the back.

"At the Incantarium. Turn back if you are afraid," Vrăja said, stopping by the iron door.

"*Afraid?* I'm not afraid," Astrid scoffed. "I just want to know where I'm—"

Vrăja cut her off. "A moment ago, I said that stories tell us who we are. There is something behind this door, and its story will tell you who *you* are. Before I open it, be sure you truly want to know."

No one turned back. Vrăja nodded, then swung the door open. As she did, the sound of chanting grew louder. A scream of rage echoed off the thick stone walls. The water was heavy with the scent of fear.

"Oh, gods," Serafina whispered as she looked into the room.

In front of her eyes, a nightmare came to life.

FORTY

IN THE CENTER of the room, the waterfire burned.

Eight river witches—incanti—swam counterclockwise around it, chanting, hands clasped, just as they had in Serafina's dream. Their faces were gray and gaunt. Blood streaked the lips of one, and dripped from the nose of another. Bruises mottled the face of a third. Sera could see that the magic cost them dearly.

Vrăja circled the witches, her eyes on the waterfire. *"Du-te înapoi, diavolul, înapoi!"* she shouted at the thing inside it. *Go back, devil, back!*

As Serafina swam closer to the witches, she saw an image rippling within the ring of waterfire. She recognized it; it was the bronze gate, sunk deep underwater and crusted with ice. Behind it, something moved with a feral grace. An eyeless face appeared at the bars. Above it rose a pair of cruel-looking, jet-black horns.

"Shokoreth!" it howled, as if it somehow knew Sera and the others had come to hear it. *"Apateón! Amăgitor!"* The monster threw itself against the gates. They shuddered and groaned. The ice encrusting them cracked. *"Daímonas tis Morsa!"*

"Aceasta le vede! Consolidarea foc! Ține-l înapoi!" Vrăja ordered. *It sees them! Strengthen the fire! Hold it back!*

The witches' voices rose. One, summoning the last of her strength, closed her eyes and leaned forward. Closer to the waterfire. Closer to the rippling image. It was a mistake.

The monster opened its lipless mouth in a snarl. As Sera watched in horror, a sinewy black arm, streaked with red, shot through the bars of the gate, through the waterfire, and into the Incantarium. The monster grabbed the witch by her throat. She screamed in pain as its nails dug into her flesh. It jerked her forward, breaking her grip on the incanti at either side of her. The waterfire went out.

"E a rupt prin! Condu-l înapoi! Închide cercul înainte să ne omoare pe toți!" Vrăja shouted. *It has broken through! Drive it back! Close the circle before it kills us all!*

There were more screams. There was blood in the water, terror and chaos in the room. Serafina was right in the midst of it, yet somehow, she was suddenly above it. Her hearing sharpened; her vision focused. She could see the monster's next move, and the one after that, as if watching pieces sweep across a chess board. And she could see how to block them.

"Becca!" she shouted. "We need a deflecto spell!"

"I'm on it!" Becca shouted, then started to songcast a protective shield.

"Ling! Take the witch's place!"

Ling joined the incanti, crossing her wrists so she could grip hands with them despite her sling. She grimaced in pain as one of the witches took hold of her bad hand, then started to chant. As she did, slender fingers of waterfire rose from the ground in front of the prison. Serafina knew the blue fire took time to conjure. She would have to draw the monster off.

"Hey!" Serafina shouted, clapping her hands loudly. "Over here!"

The monster whirled around. More hands came through the bars. In the center of each palm was a lidless eye.

"Come on! Right here, sea scum! Let's go!" Serafina shouted.

The monster released the incanta and struck at Serafina. It was fast and powerful, but Becca's deflecto, well-sung and solid, protected her.

While Serafina distracted the creature, Becca tried to pull the wounded incanta clear of the waterfire. The monster saw her.

"No!" Serafina shouted. Without thinking, she swam around the deflecto and slapped the water noisily with her tail.

The monster turned from Becca and rushed at her again. She shot backward, but not fast enough. Its claws caught her tail, opening three long gashes in it.

Serafina bit back the pain. "Ava, talk to me!" she shouted. "Can you see anything? What's it afraid of?"

"Light, Sera! It hates light!"

"Neela, frag it!"

Neela bound the lava's light tightly, then hurled it through the bars of the gates. It hit the floor and exploded, forcing the monster back. Only seconds later, though, the creature was reaching through the gate again, seemingly unharmed and fueled by a new fury. The bronze bars groaned as it shook them. One started to bend. The waterfire was rising, filling the room with blue light, but it was still weak. Becca, cradling the wounded witch, added her voice to the incanti's and the waterfire flared higher.

"It's going to get out!" Neela yelled. "The flames aren't strong enough!"

Suddenly, a blur of black and white flashed past them. It was Astrid, moving with the deadly speed of an orca. "Not if I can help it," she growled.

"Astrid, *no*! You're too close!" Serafina shouted.

But Astrid didn't listen. With a warrior's roar, she swung her sword at the monster, the muscles in her strong arms rippling. The blade came down on one of its outstretched arms and cut off a hand.

The monster shrieked in pain and fled into the depths of the prison. Its severed hand scrabbled in the silt. Astrid drove the point of her saber through it. The fingers clutched at the blade, then curled into the palm, like the legs of a dying spider.

Becca, eyes closed, songcast with all her might. As her voice rose, the flames of the waterfire leapt. Astrid backed away from it.

"Of all the *stupid* moves!" Serafina shouted at her. "You could've been killed!"

"It worked, didn't it?" Astrid shouted back.

"Songspells do, too. Ever hear of those?"

Astrid didn't reply. She swam to a wall and leaned against it, panting. She had a deep cut across one forearm. Her left temple was bleeding.

She saved our lives. All of us, Serafina thought. *Even me.* It wasn't what she expected from the daughter of the man who'd invaded Cerulea and it made her feel off-balance and unsettled.

Becca was sitting on the floor with Vrăja, who was cradling the wounded river witch.

Serafina turned her attention to them. "How is she?"

Becca shook her head. The incanta's eyes were half closed. Blood pulsed from a deep gash in her neck. She was trying to say something. Serafina bent low to listen.

". . . so many . . . in blood and fire. . . . I heard them, felt them. . . . Lost, all lost. . . . He's coming. . . . Stop him. . . ."

And then her lips stopped moving and Serafina saw the light go out of her eyes.

Vrăja raised her head; the grief in her heart was etched on her face. *"Odihnește-te acum, curajos,"* she said. *Rest now, brave one.* Sera's own heart filled with sorrow.

More Iele, drawn by the creature's roars, hurried into the Incantarium. Vrăja asked two of them to carry their sister's body away and prepare it for burial, and for another to take Ling's place in the circle and keep the chant going. And then she rose wearily. Becca helped her.

"It has been growing stronger, but I had no idea how strong until just now," Vrăja said.

"Was that—" Serafina started to say.

"Abbadon? Yes," Vrăja said.

"It's *here?* In the Incantarium?" Becca asked.

Vrăja laughed mirthlessly. "It's not supposed to be," she said. "Only its image. We watch over the monster with an *ochi*—a powerful spying spell. Abbadon broke through the ochi just now, and the waterfire, too. That is bad enough. But it also manifested physically in this room, which is far worse. Such a thing is called an *arătă*. Until now, it was a theoretical spell only. Though many have tried, no one—not even an Iele—has ever been able to cast an arătă. The monster's was weak, thank the gods. Had it been stronger, we would all be dead, not just our poor Antanasia."

"I *knew* I should have stayed outside," Neela said.

"Oh, no, bright one," Vrăja said. "If you had, I never would have seen it."

"Seen what?" Neela asked.

"How magnificent you are together," Vrăja said. "It is just as I'd hoped. It's *more* than I'd hoped. Each one of you is strong, yes, but together . . . oh, *together* your powers will become even greater. Just as theirs did."

"Excuse me?" Ling said. "*Magnificent?* One of your witches just *died*. The rest of us almost did. That thing nearly got out. If it wasn't for Astrid, it would have. We weren't magnificent. We were lucky."

"Luck has nothing to do with it. Abbadon grows strong, yes. But you will, too—now that you are united," Vrăja said.

"I don't understand," Serafina said.

"Did you not feel what happened? Did you not feel your strength? You, Serafina, marshalled your troops as cleverly as your great-grandmother, Regina Isolda, did during the War of Reykjanes Ridge. And you," she pointed at Ling, "you chanted as if you'd been born an incanta. Neela threw light as well as

I do. Becca's deflecto didn't so much as crack under Abbadon's blows. Ava saw what it fears, when we, the Iele, have not been able to. And Astrid attacked with the force of ten warriors."

Serafina looked at the others. From the expressions on their faces, she could see that they *had* felt something, just as she had. A clarity. A knowing. A new and sudden strength. It had felt so strange to feel so powerful. Disorienting. And a little bit scary. *How had it happened?* she wondered.

"You will do even more. We will teach you," Vrăja said, swimming toward the door. "Come! There is much to do. We will go back to my chambers now. We will—"

"No," Astrid said, putting her sword back in its scabbard. "I'm not going anywhere. Not until you tell us why you brought us here."

Vrăja stopped. She turned, fixing Astrid with her bright black eyes. "To finish what you just began," she said.

"Finish *what*? I don't get it. You want me to cut off more of the monster's hands?"

"No, child," she said.

"Good," Astrid said, looking relieved. "Because that was really tough."

"I want you to cut off its head."

FORTY-ONE

ASTRID'S LAUGHTER rang out above the witches' chanting.

"*Cut off its head!* That's a good one, Baba Vrăja. I mean, did you see that thing? It's really strong and really mad. If it could have, it would've cut off *our* heads. So really, why did you summon us here?" she asked.

Vrăja was not laughing.

"Wait, you're not . . . You *can't* be serious."

"I've never been more serious. You must go to the Southern Sea, where the monster lies imprisoned. Another seeks it for dark purposes. This other has woken it. You must find the monster and kill it before this other can free it. If you do not, the seas, and all in them, will fall to Abbadon."

Serafina was speechless. They all were. The six mermaids looked at each other in wide-eyed disbelief, then all started talking at once.

"Go to the Southern Sea?" Ling said.

"We'll freeze to death!" Becca said.

"Kill Abbadon?" Ava said.

"How would we even *find* him? The Southern Sea is huge!" Neela said.

"This is totally insane," Astrid said. "I'm out of here."

As Serafina watched Astrid swim toward the door, lines from her nightmare suddenly came back to her.

> *Gather now from seas and rivers,*
> *Become one mind, one heart, one bond*
> *Before the waters, and all creatures in them,*
> *Are laid to waste by Abbadon!*

And suddenly she knew what she had to do. Just as she had moments ago, when the monster attacked them. She had to keep the group together, no matter what. *One mind, one heart, one bond.* She couldn't let anyone leave.

"Astrid, wait," she said.

Astrid snorted. "Later," she said.

"You're afraid," Serafina said, sensing that the only way to stop her was to challenge her.

She was right. Astrid stopped dead, then turned around, eyes blazing.

"What did you say?"

"I said, you're afraid. You're afraid of the story. That's why you want to leave."

"Afraid of what story? What are you *talking* about? You're as crazy as she is," Astrid said, nodding at Vrăja.

Serafina turned to the river witch. "Baba Vrăja, before you opened the door to this room, you said that what's inside it had a story," she said. "And that it would tell us who we are. We need to hear that story. *Now.*"

FORTY-TWO

THREE EYEBALLS, set in three amber rings, twisted around in their settings and stared at Serafina.

Serafina stared back uneasily.

"You like them?" Vrăja asked, as she handed her a cup and saucer.

"They're very, um, unusual," Sera replied.

Vrăja had led the mermaids back to her study. She'd invited them all to sit down, and had sent a servant for a pot of tea.

"They're terragogg eyes," she said now.

"Did they drown or something?" Neela asked.

"Or something," Vrăja said. She smiled and Serafina noticed, for the first time, that her teeth were very sharp. "One dumped oil into my river. Another killed an otter. The third bulldozed trees where osprey nested. They live still—or rather, *exist*—as *cadavru*. I use them as sentries."

"That rotter by the mouth of the Olt, is he one?" Neela asked.

"Yes. He has his right eye and I have his left. What he sees, I see. Very handy when death riders are about."

She finished pouring the tea and sat on the edge of her desk.

She'd poured a cup for herself, but didn't drink it. Instead she picked up a piece of smooth, flat stone that was lying next to the teapot and turned it over in her hands. Symbols were carved into its surface.

"The songspell to make a cadavru is called a *trezi*. A Romanian spell. Very old," she said. "I have many such spells. Passed down from obârşie to obârşie. These spells are how we, the Order of the Iele, have endured as long as we have. Merrow created us four thousand years ago, and we have carried out the duties she entrusted to us ever since, in order to protect the merfolk."

"From what?" Ling asked.

Vrăja smiled. "Ourselves."

She held the stone out so that Sera, Neela, Astrid, Becca, and Ling could see it, then handed it to Ava, so she could feel it. Baby, dozing in his mistress's lap, growled in his sleep.

"Did you know that this writing is nearly forty centuries old?" Vrăja asked. "It came from a Minoan temple. It's one of the few surviving records of Atlantis. It—like Plato's accounts, and those of other ancients—Posidonius, Hellanicus, Philo—tells us that the island sank because of natural causes." She looked at the mermaids, then said, "It lies."

"Why?" Ava asked.

"Because that's what Merrow wanted the world to know about Atlantis—lies. Stories have great power. Stories endure. Merrow knew that, so she had everything that told the true story of Atlantis expunged."

"But why would she do that?" Neela asked.

"The truth was too dangerous," Vrăja said. "Merrow had seen her people—men and women, little children—swallowed by fire and water. You see, it wasn't an earthquake or a volcano that doomed Atlantis, as you undoubtedly have been taught. Those were only the mechanisms of its ruin. It was one of the island's own who destroyed it."

"Baba Vrăja, how do you know this?" Serafina asked. She was mesmerized by the witch's words. Ancient Atlantean history was her passion. All her life, she had hungered to know more about the lost island, but there were so few conchs from the period, so little information to be had.

"We know from Merrow herself. She gave the truth to the first obârșie in a bloodsong. The obârșie kept it in her heart. On her deathbed, she passed it to her successor, and so on. We are forbidden to speak of it unless the monster rises. For four thousand years, we have been silent."

"Until now," Ling said.

"Yes," Vrăja said. "Until now. But I have begun at the end, and beginnings are much better places to start. *Whatever you do or dream you can do—begin it. Boldness has genius and power and magic in it.* A terragogg wrote that. Some say it was the poet Goethe. He could have been writing about Atlantis for that was Atlantis—a *boldness*. A place made of genius and magic. Ah, such magic!" she said, smiling. "Nothing could compare to it. Athens? A backwater. Rome? A dusty hill town. Thebes? A watering hole. Mines of copper, tin, silver, and gold made Atlantis wealthy. Fertile soil made it fruitful. Bountiful waters fed its people. This island paradise was governed by mages—"

"The Six Who Ruled," Becca said.

"Yes. Orfeo, Merrow, Sycorax, Navi, Pyrrha, and Nyx. Their great magic came from the gods, who had given each of them a powerful talisman. They were very close, the greatest of friends, and their powers were never stronger than when they were together. They ruled Atlantis wisely and well, and were revered for it. No decision involving the welfare of the people was made without the agreement of all six. No judgment or sentence was passed. There was a prison on the island—the Carceron. It was built of huge, interlocking stone blocks and had heavy bronze gates fitted with an ingenious lock. The gates could not be opened to admit a prisoner, or free one, unless the talismans of all six mages had been fitted into the lock's six keyholes."

Vrăja paused to take a sip of her tea. "No society is perfect," she continued, setting the cup back into its saucer, "but Atlantis was just and peaceful. At the time, it was thought that this island civilization would last forever."

"What happened? Why didn't it?" Serafina asked, listening raptly to Vrăja's every word.

"We do not know entirely. Merrow would not tell the first obârşie. All she would say is that Orfeo had been lost to them, that he'd turned his back on his duties and his people to create Abbadon, a monster whose powers rivaled the gods'. How he made it and of what, she would not say. The other five mages tried to stop him and a battle ensued. Orfeo unleashed his monster and Atlantis was destroyed. Abbadon shook the earth until it cracked open. Lava poured forth, the seas churned, and the dying island sank beneath the waves."

Serafina sat back in her chair, silently shaking her head.

"You don't believe me, child?" Vrăja asked.

"I don't know what to believe," she replied. "How could Abbadon shake the earth? How could it churn the seas? How could anything be that powerful?"

Vrăja took a deep breath. She touched her fingers to her chest and drew a bloodsong, groaning in pain as she did, for it wasn't a skein of blood that came from her heart, but a torrent. It whirled through the room with malevolent force, tearing conchs off the shelves, smashing stone jars, turning the waters as dark as night.

Sound and color spun together violently and then the mermaids saw it—the ruin of Atlantis. People ran shrieking through the streets of Elysia, the capital, as the ground trembled and buildings fell all around them. Bodies were everywhere. Smoke and ash filled the air. Lava flowed down a flight of stone steps. A child, too small to walk, sat at the bottom of them, screaming in terror, her mother dead beside her. A man ran to the girl and snatched her up. Seconds later, the cobblestones upon which she'd sat were submerged by molten rock.

"Run!" a woman's voice shouted. "Get into the water! Hurry! It's coming this way." Scores of people ran toward the sea. "Help them, please . . . oh, great Neria, stop this bloodshed!"

Serafina couldn't see the woman who'd shouted, but she knew who she was—Merrow, her ancestor. This was Merrow's memory.

Serafina heard the monster first. Its voice was that of a thousand voices, all shrieking at once. The sound was so harrowing, it flattened her against her chair. Then she saw the creature.

It was a living darkness, glazed in dusky red. Shaped like a man, it had two legs, and many arms. Powerful muscles gave it strength and speed. Its sightless horned head whipped around, drawn by the sound of running feet, of cries and screams. Hideous hands with eyes sunk into their palms guided the creature. It slashed at the helpless people trying to escape. When it killed, it threw its head back, opened its lipless pit of a mouth, and roared.

"Merrow!" a voice called out.

A man appeared, stumbling through the devastated streets. He was slender and dark-skinned, with blind eyes. He wore a linen tunic, sandals, and a large ruby ring. He had Ava's high cheekbones and her long black braids.

"Nyx!" Merrow said, rushing to him. "Thank gods you're all right! Where is he?"

"He's barricaded himself inside the Temple of Morsa."

"We have to get his talisman. And everyone else's. If we can get them all, we can open the Carceron and force the monster inside."

"He'll never surrender it. We'd have to kill him to get it."

"Then we will."

"Merrow, *no*. This is *Orfeo*."

"There's no other way, Nyx! He'll kill *us*. Find Navi. I'll get Sycorax and Pyrrha. Meet us at the temple."

And then the bloodsong faded and the waters cleared and the six mermaids sat in their chairs, shaken and silent.

Vrăja was the first to speak. "Nyx was killed by Abbadon before he could get to the temple, but he'd found Navi. She was badly injured, but she made it to the temple with Nyx's talisman and her own. Merrow managed to corner Orfeo, kill him, and take his talisman. The surviving mages succeeded in driving Abbadon into the Carceron, but Navi and Pyrrha were killed in the struggle. As soon as the monster was locked away, Merrow took the talismans out of the lock, then led her people into the water. Sycorax, with the help of a thousand whales, dragged the Carceron to the Southern Sea and sank it under the ice. She died there. The whales sang her to her grave. And ever since, Abbadon has slept buried under the ice. Forgotten. Lost to time. But now it stirs. Now someone is trying to free it. And already it makes its evil presence felt. Realms wage war. Mer die. The waters turn red with blood. And now you must destroy it. You must gather the six talismans, use them to open the Carceron, then go inside and kill it."

"Baba Vrăja, why us?" Serafina asked. "Why have you summoned *us*, six teenage merls, to kill Abbadon? Why not emperors or admirals or commanders with their soldiers? Why not the waters' most powerful mages?"

Vrăja looked at them each in turn, then said, "You *are* the most powerful mages. There have been none as powerful in four thousand years. Not since the Six Who Ruled."

"Ooooo-*kay*. I thought you were nuts. Now I know you are," Astrid said.

"One of you knows this to be true. One of you sees it," said Vrăja.

The mermaids looked at each other. They all wore confused expressions except for Ava, who was nodding.

"Do you see something, Ava?" Serafina asked. "What is it?"

"I don't know why I didn't see it before," Ava said.

"See *what*?" Astrid said. "No one here's a canta magus. This is *crazy*!"

"No, it's not," Ava said. "It makes perfect sense. There *were* six. There *are* six. Six of them, six of us."

Becca's eyebrows shot up. "Wait, you're saying . . . no *way*, Ava. It *can't* be."

"But it is," Vrăja said. "You six are the direct descendants of the six greatest mages who ever lived. Heiresses to their powers. Merrow, Orfeo, Sycorax, Navi, Pyrrha, Nyx . . . The Six Who Ruled live on inside each of *you*."

FORTY-THREE

ASTRID BLINKED.

Ava's jaw dropped.

Becca and Ling shook their heads.

Neela turned bright blue.

Serafina spoke.

"Baba Vrăja, how can we be heiresses to the powers of the greatest mages who ever lived? It doesn't make sense. Astrid's right—we'd all be canta magi with perfect voices."

Vrăja smiled. "You forget the canta magi are mer, and mer-people's powers are in their voices. The goddess Neria made it so when she transformed the Atlanteans. She strengthened our voices so they would carry in water. But Merrow and her fellow mages—your ancestors—were born human. Human magic takes different forms. Some of your powers may, too. The abilities you demonstrated while fighting Abbadon certainly suggest they do. Neela and Becca cast songspells against Abbadon. Ling chanted. But you didn't sing, Serafina. Neither did Astrid or Ava. Your powers may be a mix of your mage ancestors' human magic and your own sea magic."

"Who's descended from whom?" Ava asked. "Serafina's descended from Merrow, of course, but what about the rest of us?"

"A very good question," Vrăja said. "Never before have six direct descendants been of the same age at the same time—just as the original six were." She walked toward Serafina and put her hands on her shoulders. "As you said, Ava, Serafina is the daughter of Merrow. She was a great leader—brave and just. And a very powerful mage. Her greatest power, however, was love."

"Love?" Astrid scoffed. "How is *that* a power?"

"Nothing is more powerful than love," Vrăja said.

"Oh, no? How about a JK-67 lava-bomb launcher?"

"You have much to learn," Vrăja said to Astrid. "Even your lava-bomb launcher could not have saved us today. Only Serafina's quick thinking could. She would have sacrificed herself for all of you. A willingness to lay down one's life for others is born of love."

"Or stupidity," Astrid said.

It was Neela's turn next.

"One who holds the light," Vrăja said to her. "You are the daughter of Navi. She was a wealthy woman who had come to Atlantis from the land we now call India. Kind and good-hearted, she used her riches to build hospitals, orphanages, and homes for the poor. It was said she could hold light in her hands, as well as her heart. She could pull down light from the moon and stars, and like them, she gave her people hope in their darkest hours."

Neela looked doubtful. "Baba Vrăja, I don't know how much of Navi's power I've inherited. I mean, sometimes I can cast a decent frag, other times I can barely get a bunch of moon jellies to light up."

"There's an explanation for that. I believe that your powers—and those of your friends—strengthen when you're in proximity to one another," Vrăja said. "How do you think you and Serafina managed to flee into the looking glass at the duca's palazzo? There are canta magi who can't do that."

"You may be right," Neela said. "My songspells are always better when I'm around Sera."

Vrăja raised an eyebrow. "I *may* be right?" she said. "Try to do again what you did in the Incantarium."

Neela looked around self-consciously. She took a deep breath and sang a fragor lux spell. This time, the light bomb she whirled across the room took a chunk out of the wall.

"Whoa," she whispered, wide-eyed. "How did that . . . how did I . . ."

"Magic begets magic," Vrăja said.

Becca was next.

"*One with spirit sure and strong.* Just like your ancestor Pyrrha," Vrăja said to her. "She was a brilliant military commander—one of the greatest. She came from the shores of Atlantica. You are like her."

"That can't be right," Becca said. "I'm just a student. With an after-school job at Baudel's. I plan to major in business when I go to college so I can open my own shop one day. I have a lot of ideas for songpearls, but I don't know a thing about soldiering."

"Pyrrha started out as an artisan, too—a blacksmith. She could bid fire. She had a forge on Atlantis, as you have at Baudel's," Vrăja explained. "One day, she saw enemy ships coming and sent a boy on horseback to the capital, to alert them. Calling up the fire in her forge, she quickly transformed farm tools into weapons and armed everyone in her village. As the invaders marched through it, the villagers ambushed them and held them until troops from Elysia arrived. Pyrrha helped save Atlantis with her quick thinking. As you helped save us today, with your ability to call waterfire."

"I never knew I had that ability," said Becca. "Not until today."

Vrăja then swam to Ava. "You are a daughter of Nyx. He came from the shores of a great river now known as the Mississippi. Like you, he was blind. And like you, he felt the things he could not see. Just as a bat does on land, or a shark in the water. Magic strengthened his gift, so that he could not only see what it is, but what will be. It will do the same for you."

After Vrăja finished with Ava, there were two mermaids left—Ling and Astrid.

"Now for the big fat question: Who is Orfeo's descendant?" Astrid said. "Let me guess . . . it's *not* Ling."

"Sycorax is Ling's ancestor," Vrăja said. "She came from eastern China, on the shores of Qin. She was born an omnivoxa, and her magical powers strengthened her gift. She could speak not just many languages, but *every* language. And not only human tongues, but those of animals, birds, creatures of the sea, trees, and flowers. She was Atlantis's supreme justice. She solved disputes between citizens and negotiated treaties between realms. She was very wise."

Ling smiled, but it was tinged with bitterness. "When I was little, people said I was a liar because I told them I could hear anemones talking. Plankton. Even kelp. I don't have to study a language to know it. I only have to hear it. I've never known why. Now I do," she said.

Astrid sat glaring the whole time Ling was speaking. "So *I'm* Orfeo's descendant. That's just perfect. So, like, *I'm* the bad guy, right?" she asked angrily, after Ling had finished.

"Orfeo was a healer. His people loved him. He was a musician, too, and played the lyre to soothe the sick and suffering. He came from Greenland. Of the six mages who ruled Atlantis, Orfeo was the greatest. His powers were unsurpassed. As yours may be, child."

Astrid laughed harshly. "You're wrong, Vrăja. *So* wrong. It's not true. Orfeo's *not* my ancestor. The whole idea is totally ridiculous. I mean, if you only *knew* . . ."

"Knew what?" Vrăja asked.

"Never mind. Just forget it," Astrid said. "I can't be part of this nutty little playdate any longer. The realms are on the verge of war, in case you haven't noticed. I'm going home to make myself useful."

"You *can't* leave," Serafina said, in spite of the distrust she felt for Astrid. "We're supposed to be six, just like the Six Who Ruled—not five. Vrăja said our powers *put together* would be extraordinary. There's no hope of defeating the monster without *all* of us."

"I have news for you. There's no hope of defeating it *with* all of us. We're six kids! The only ones dreaming are *them*." She hooked her thumb in Vrăja's direction. "They need to stop their bogus chanting, raise an army, and go after this thing."

"One who does not yet believe," Vrăja said.

"You're right about that," Astrid said. "I *don't* believe. I don't believe I came here. I don't believe I wasted my time on this. I don't believe I'm listening to this nonsense—"

"Excuse me." It was Becca. Her voice, unlike Sera's and Astrid's, was calm and unruffled. "This isn't helping us make any progress. Where, exactly, *is* the Carceron?" she asked, taking a piece of kelp parchment and a squid ink pen out of her traveling case.

"All we know is that it's somewhere in the Southern Sea," Vrăja replied.

"Well, *that* narrows it down," Astrid said.

Becca jotted down a few notes, then asked, "What are the talismans?"

"We don't know," Vrăja said. "Merrow did not reveal them to us. We believe she hid them so no one could ever use them to free Abbadon."

"If she was so worried about the possibility, why didn't she destroy them?"

"Because they are indestructible. They were given by the gods."

"Any ideas where she hid them?"

"No," Vrăja said.

"Of course not!" Astrid said. "Why do you keep asking questions, Becca? You're not getting any answers! Don't you ever give up?"

Becca's glasses had slipped down her nose. She pushed them back up. "No, Astrid, I don't." She turned back to Vrăja. "And Abbadon—any ideas what it might be made of?" Becca asked.

"It looked like it was made of darkness, but how could that be?" Ling asked.

"Only Orfeo has the answer to your questions, and he's been dead for four thousand years. Not even the five mages who fought Abbadon knew. That's why they couldn't kill him," Vrăja replied.

"The most powerful magi of all time couldn't kill Abbadon, but *we're* supposed to?" Astrid said.

"Ever hear of positive thinking, *mina*?" Ava asked testily.

"Ever hear of *rational* thinking? How are we supposed to kill it? Sneak up on it? It has like, a dozen hands! With eyes in them! We'll never even get close to it," Astrid said.

"So what should we do? Just go home? Go shoaling, go shopping? Pretend none of this ever happened?" Ling asked heatedly.

"*Yes!*" Astrid shouted.

"Wait, calm down, everyone. Let's take a deep breath and look at what we know," Becca said.

"Which is, umm, hold on, let me see . . . *nothing*!" Astrid said. "We don't know what the talismans are. Or where they are. We don't know exactly where the monster is or what it is."

"We do know—" Becca began.

"That we're going to get our wrasses kicked!" Astrid said. "Abbadon killed thousands of people! He sank an entire island!"

"I would appreciate it if you would stop interrupting me," Becca said.

"And I would appreciate it if you would stop being mental."

"You're unbelievably rude."

"You're clueless."

"Stop arguing, *please*," Serafina said, trying to hold the group together. "It's not helping."

"You're right, it's not," Astrid said. "So, hey, let's just poison everybody. Problem solved. Isn't that how they do things in your neck of the water?"

"Whoa!" Ling said. "Time *out!*"

"Astrid, you are *totally* out of line!" Ava said.

But Astrid didn't listen. And Serafina, infuriated, started tossing insults back at her. And everyone else just talked louder. A few minutes later, they were all arguing, shouting, and flipping their tail fins at one another.

"I grow tired. I shall leave you now," Vrăja suddenly said, the sound of defeat in her voice. "The novices have prepared food for you, and beds." She turned to go.

"Thank you, Baba Vrăja, but I won't need a bed. I'm heading out," Astrid said.

Vrăja spun around. Her eyes bored into Astrid. "Orfeo had great powers, child. The greatest the world has ever seen. He had to choose how to use them. He chose evil. Magic is what you make it."

Astrid's angry expression cracked. It fell from her face like ice off a glacier, revealing raw fear. "But Baba Vrăja, you don't understand! I *can't* choose!" she said.

It was too late. Vrăja was gone. The doors closed behind her.

The six mermaids were by themselves.

FORTY-FOUR

SERAFINA LOOKED AT ASTRID. "What was *that* about?" she asked.

"Nothing," Astrid said brusquely. "It's been real, merls. Good luck with it all."

She tried to swim out of Vrăja's study, but two armed frogs blocked her. They waited until she stopped shouting, then one of them spoke.

"Can you tell me what he said?" Astrid asked Ling.

"So sorry. I don't speak Tĭngjŭ."

"Tĭngjŭ? What does that mean? The guards don't speak Tĭngjŭ. They speak Amphobos."

Ling smiled tightly. "Tĭngjŭ means *jerk*. And I wasn't talking about the guards."

"Sorry," Astrid said stiffly. "Can you *please* tell me what he said?"

"He said, 'You will stay, as Baba Vrăja instructed. There is danger in the darkness. You will be safe here.'"

"Safe . . . yeah, sure," Astrid muttered, looking pointedly at Serafina. "As long as I don't eat anything."

Serafina said nothing, but her fins flared.

A young river witch appeared and led the mermaids to a suite of rooms. One contained a round stone dining table and chairs, another beds. Two more witches brought food and the six mermaids sat down to eat a late supper. The food was simple, but fresh and delicious—salted frogs' eggs, pickled water spiders, plump leeches in algae sauce, and a salad of marsh grass topped with crunchy water beetles.

Sera was quiet during the meal, overwhelmed the enormity of what she'd learned in Vrăja's study, and what she'd witnessed in the Incantarium.

As she ate, she realized that everything she'd been taught about the origins of her people was a lie. Merrow had sought to protect the mer by wiping out all traces of the truth of their beginnings, but instead she'd left them dangerously vulnerable to the very evil she'd tried to defeat.

Merrow, the first regina, a mermaid so revered that in the minds of the mer that she was seen as infallible, had made a mistake. A big one. And now it was up to herself and five other teenagers to put it right.

Sera remembered the towering statue of her ancestor that had stood in the grounds of the palace. She saw herself, as she had been only weeks ago, looking up at Merrow. Looking up *to* Merrow. That merl, dressed in a beautiful silk gown, surrounded by Janiçari, protected from the cruelties of the world by her powerful mother, seemed so innocent and naive to her now, a child—one who'd lived in a world made for her, not by her. By decisions made for her. Under Merrow's many decrees.

Part of Sera still felt like that child, and still longed for the strength and wisdom of her mother. But another, braver part realized that childhood was over and that she'd have to find her own way through this, just as she'd been finding her way ever since she'd fled Cerulea.

When everyone had finished eating, Ava fed the scraps to Baby. Serafina, Neela, and Becca cleared the dishes. Ling took out the letter tiles Lena had given her and started making words with them. Astrid pulled a caballabong ball out of her satchel, and started bouncing it against a wall, keeping up a steady *thwak thwak thwak*.

Neela cast a songspell to turn up the light in the dining room. Instead of brightening, though, the lava globes promptly dimmed.

"Oops," she said, looking embarrassed.

"One who keeps the light!" Ling said, in a spooky voice.

"Descended from the great mage Navi!" Becca chimed in.

Serafina restored the light and everyone cracked up, including Neela. But the laughter was short-lived. Neela suddenly lowered her face into her hands, and said, "Oh, gods. It's *not* funny. It's so *not*. One who keeps the light? *Please.* What if we find the Carceron and instead of unleashing a frag on Abbadon, I dim the lights?"

"I know," Ling said, rearranging her letter tiles with her good hand. "I'm worried about the same thing. I mean, how will my great powers of language help defeat the monster? What am I supposed to do? Reason with him?"

"Tell him to use his words," Neela joked.

Ava, giggling at that, choked on her drink. Her noisy snarf made the others giggle too.

"You could tell him that bullying is totally unacceptable," Becca suggested.

"Or that he needs to start making good choices," Sera said.

"Tell Crabby Abby he's going to sit on the naughty chair if he sinks one more island," Astrid said, catching her ball.

The other five looked at her, astonished, then they all burst into loud, hysterical laughter and couldn't stop. Becca laughed so hard, she snorted like a walrus. Serafina wheezed. Ava held her sides. Ling had tears in her eyes. Neela turned sky blue.

"Astrid, you're funny," Ling said when the laughter had subsided. "Who knew?"

"Don't tell anyone," Astrid said, bouncing her ball again.

"Ah, *gatinhas*," Ava said. "How do we do this? Where do we start?"

"Excellent questions," Becca said.

"How do we find out what the talismans are? And where they are?" Neela asked.

"Before Traho does," Serafina added.

"Who's Traho?" Becca asked.

Serafina glanced at Astrid, searching her face for some tell-tale sign—a twitch, a widening of the eyes—that might betray her knowledge of this merman. But Astrid gave none. Either she truly didn't know him or she was an excellent actress.

"Traho and the Ondalinians attacked Miromara," Sera explained.

"I wouldn't go there if I were you," Astrid warned.

Sera ignored her. "They captured Neela and me and held us prisoner. Traho knows about the nightmare, the chant, and the Iele. He wanted the names of the other mermaids who'd been summoned. And he wanted to know if any of us had already found any talismans."

"What did you tell him?"

"That I didn't know what he was talking about. Which didn't go over well. He threatened to cut my fingers off, so I gave him fake names. Luckily, we escaped before he could check them out."

"Does Traho know what the talismans are?"

"I think so. If he didn't, he would have asked me. He only asked *where* they are."

"But how could he know what they are? Not even the Iele know that," Ling said, still concentrating on her letter tiles.

"Good point," Sera conceded. "But he's after them, so he *must* know."

"Even if we were to find the talismans and get to the Southern Sea before this Traho does, we have no idea how to kill the monster," Becca said.

"Because it can't be killed. I'll say it again: Merrow and her fellow mages couldn't do it. What makes you think we can?" Astrid asked.

What's she afraid of? Serafina wondered. *She fought Abbadon like a tiger shark. How can someone that tough be afraid of anything?*

"It's not question of *can* we," Ling said. "You saw what that thing did to Atlantis. It'll do it again if it gets out. We have to stop asking ourselves 'Can we do this?' and 'Should we do this?' There's only one question we need to ask . . . *how.*"

Becca nodded. "Ling's right," she said. She pulled out the piece of parchment she'd written notes on earlier and looked it over. "We can't do anything until we find the talismans."

"True," Ava said.

"So we have to backtrack. We have to progress logically from the fall of Atlantis, when the talismans were last used . . ."

Progress. The word pushed at Serafina's mind. *Why?* She turned the word over and over in her head, sensing that it was important somehow, but unable to grasp how it connected to Abbadon, the Carceron, or the talismans.

". . . to the rise of Miromara, Merrow's realm. Then we progress to . . ."

Progress . . . Merrow . . .

"Becca, that's it!" Serafina shouted. "Her *progress*—Merrow's Progress! You're a genius!"

"I am?" Becca said, startled.

"Do you know what the talismans are, Sera? Or where Merrow hid them?" Ava asked.

"No, I don't know the *what* or the *where.* I wish I did. But merls, I think I know the *when.*"

FORTY-FIVE

SERAFINA WAS SO EXCITED, she was talking a million words a minute.

"I'm working on a term conch on Merrow's Progress," she said. "I mean I *was* working on it. Before Cerulea was attacked. I've spent hours in the Ostrokon—"

"Wait, Sera, slow down!" Ling said. "What's a progress?"

Serafina explained. "Ten years after Atlantis was destroyed, Merrow made a journey throughout the waters of the world. She said she was scouting out safe places for the merfolk to live. Her people were thriving and she knew they would need more space than Miromara could offer. She took a handful of her ministers with her and a few servants. It was the *only time* in her entire reign that she left Miromara."

"You think she was really hiding the talismans?" said Ava.

"I do."

"Why wouldn't she hide them in Miromara?" Astrid asked.

"Too risky. There were always courtiers around. Someone would have seen her," Serafina said. "As I was saying, Cerulea's Ostrokon has a large collection of conchs on Merrow's Progress.

I've listened to about twenty so far, but there are way more than that. Maybe one of them can tell us exactly where she went. And the most dangerous places she visited. That's where she would've hidden the talismans."

Astrid gave her a skeptical look. "But Merrow could've hidden the talismans anywhere."

"I *know* that, Astrid. But it's something. It's a start," Serafina said.

"Merls! Here's another one!" Ling said, pointing at her letter tiles. "Look!" She'd spelled out three separate words: *shokoreth*, *apateón*, and *amăgitor.*

"Look at what? It's all nonsense," Astrid said.

"That's what I thought, too. But they're real words—words that Abbadon said. I thought it was just making monster noises. But it's not. It's talking. The first word is Arabic, the second Greek, the third Romanian. They all mean the same thing—*deceiver.*"

"Why would it say the same word over and over again, and in different languages?" Becca asked.

"I don't know. These words here"—she pointed to another row of tiles—"*Daímonas tis Morsa*—mean *demon of Morsa.*"

"Morsa's an old goddess, right?" Ava said. "No one really talks about her."

"She's a seriously dark goddess," Ling said. "The old myths say she was the scavenger goddess, and took the form of a jackal. It was the job of Horok, the ancient coelecanth god, to carry the souls of the dead to the underworld, and it was Morsa's job to take away their bodies. But Morsa wanted more power, so she started practicing necromancy. She planned to make an army of the dead and overthrow Neria. Neria found out and was furious. She punished Morsa by giving her the face of death and the body of a serpent. Then she placed a crown of scorpions on her head and banished her."

"Wow. That's *cold*. Moral of the story? Never mess with Neria," Neela said.

"There was a temple built to Morsa on Atlantis," Serafina said.

"It might tell us more," Becca offered. "If only we could get to it."

"Fat chance. It's surrounded by Opafago. They'd rip your head off before you got within five leagues of the place," Astrid said.

"Why is that? I've always wondered. Why is it that a bunch of bloodthirsty cannibals was allowed to take over the ruins of Atlantis?" Neela asked.

"Because Merrow forced them into the Barrens of Thira, the waters around Atlantis," Serafina explained. "The Opafago lived in Miromara and hunted mer. Merrow wanted that stopped, so she used her acqua guerrieri to encircle them and herd them into the Barrens."

"Merrow didn't think that one through, did she?" Neela mused. "It's the most important archaeological site to the mer, but because of the Opafago, we can't even set fin in it."

"I thought that, too," Serafina said. "I thought it was just another one of her unfathomable decrees. Until Vrăja told us how

Atlantis was really destroyed. According to historians, Merrow *said* she put the Opafago in the waters around Atlantis because she needed somewhere to put them and the ruins were . . . well, ruins, and useless. But now I think she settled the Opafago there on purpose. To prevent anyone from ever exploring them."

"In case they learned the truth," Ava said.

"Exactly. There are clues we need in those ruins, I'm sure of it. If only we could get to them," Serafina said.

"The Opafago eat their victims alive, you know," said Astrid. "While their heart's still beating and their blood's still pumping. The flesh is juicier that way."

"What a ray of light you are," Ling said. She got up from the table. "We can't get to Atlantis, but we *can* observe Abbadon. And I'm going to do just that. First thing tomorrow. Ava saw that it hates light. I need to find out if it has other weaknesses. I got something out of it today. *Deceiver.* It's not much. It's not a talisman. But like Sera said, it's a start."

She yawned and told the others she was turning in. Becca, Neela, and Ava were right behind her. Sera didn't join them. She wasn't tired. She was busy thinking.

Astrid had gone back to bouncing her caballabong ball. "How are you going to do all this, Serafina? How are you going to get into your Ostrokon to listen to conchs when Cerulea's occupied? How are you going to get into Atlantis? How are you going to kill Abbadon?"

"I don't know yet, but maybe I can get help. If I can find my uncle, and my brother, they may have ideas. If my mother's still alive—"

Astrid cut her off. "If, if, if," she said. "This *isn't* a start. It's an end. You're going to get yourself killed." She glanced in the direction of the bedroom. "And you're going to get *them* killed too. This whole thing's a joke." She threw her ball harder. "And here's another one . . . me being a descendant of Orfeo's, the greatest mage who ever lived."

Astrid said those last words to herself, but Serafina heard them. *Why can't she accept that Orfeo's her ancestor? Is it because of what he did? Or is there more to it?* she wondered.

"Hey, Astrid . . . Baba Vrăja's right, you know. Magic is what you make it. Just because Orfeo was evil doesn't mean you are. Evil isn't inherited. Like eye color or something."

Astrid stopped bouncing her ball. She looked at Serafina. "It's not that. I mean, having Orfeo in your family coral branch is *totally* lowtide, but . . ."

"But what?"

Astrid shook her head.

"Astrid, what is it?"

"Nothing. Really. Forget it."

"Okay. Forgotten."

Serafina, frustrated by Astrid's unwillingness to talk, scooped the tiles Ling had left on the table into their bag. She picked up the stray cups and put them on a tray.

Astrid bounced her ball harder.

"It wasn't us," she said suddenly. She whirled around to face Serafina. The ball went flying across the room. "I want you to know that. Ondalina *didn't* invade Miromara. We didn't attack

Cerulea. We didn't send an assassin. My father would *never* do such a thing. He would never hurt Isabella or Bastiaan or the Matalis. He values them, and the peace between our realms, too highly. His own sister lives in Miromara. In Tsarno, as you know. He wouldn't risk her life."

Serafina weighed Astrid's words, then she said, "He broke the permutavi, though. It's been honored by both kingdoms for a hundred years. You were supposed to come to Miromara and Desiderio was supposed to go to Ondalina. Just like your aunt Sigurlin and my uncle Ludovico did at the last permutavi. Why did he break it?"

Astrid sat down across from Serafina. "There are reasons," she said. "If you knew . . . if I could tell you . . ." Her hands, resting on top of the table, knotted into fists. Her long blond hair, pale as moonlight, swirled around her shoulders. Her ice-blue eyes sought Serafina's. In them, Serafina could see a yearning to talk, to share what was troubling her.

"Astrid, seriously, Abbadon's the enemy, you know? Not me. Not Miromara," Serafina said, surprised by her own sudden desire to talk to this difficult merl. "We didn't send any assassins either. The last thing my mother wants is war. Not for her people, not for yours. You said there were reasons why Ondalina broke the permutavi—what are they? Tell me."

Serafina held Astrid's gaze. For a few seconds, she was certain Astrid would confide in her. But instead of talking, Astrid brusquely pushed back her chair and rose.

"I can't," she said helplessly. "I just *can't*." She swam toward the bedroom. When she got to the door, she turned back to Serafina. "I'm sorry," she said. And then she was gone.

Serafina looked at the empty space of the doorway. "Yeah," she said softly. "Me too."

FORTY-SIX

"**S**HE'S GONE," Serafina said angrily.

She'd just swum into Vrăja's study. It was early the next morning.

"Are you surprised?" Vrăja asked. She was sitting in her chair of bones and antlers, wearing a dress the color of oxblood. Its high neckline was trimmed with tiny bird skulls, its bodice beaded with hawk talons, wolves' teeth, and polished bits of turtle shell.

"You knew?"

"I heard her leave early this morning."

"Why didn't you stop her?"

"How? Should I have taken her prisoner? There *was* no stopping her," Vrăja said. "She does not wish to be here. Sit down, child."

Serafina sat in the chair opposite her. "We're supposed to be the Six," she said.

"It looks like you are now the Five," Vrăja said.

"How can we destroy the monster without her?"

"I don't know. But then again, I don't know how you would have done it *with* her."

299

"She's scared," Serafina said.

"You would have to be mad *not* to be scared of Abbadon."

"I don't think she's scared of Abbadon. I mean, any more than the rest of us are. It's something else that she's swimming from. I don't know what it is."

"Is it Astrid you speak of, or yourself?" Vrăja asked shrewdly.

Serafina looked at her as if she hadn't heard her correctly. "Um, *Astrid*," she said. "Because *she's* the one who's swimming away."

"So are you, child."

"No, I'm not!" Serafina said. "I *stayed*, Baba Vrăja. Right here with the others. We're making our plans. Trying to figure this all out. Ling's on her way to listen to Abbadon, to try to decipher more of its words. Becca's asking the witch who brought our breakfast how to cast an ochi. Neela's practicing her light bombs—"

Vrăja cut her off. "And you?"

"I'm plotting a route to the Kobolds' waters. To see if the rumors are true and my uncle is there. And to find out whatever I can about my mother and brother. With their help, maybe I can get back to Cerulea. And the Ostrokon. So I can listen to conchs on Merrow's Progress. We think she hid the talismans during that journey. The conchs might give us clues as to where."

"Merrow's Progress . . . excellent thinking," Vrăja said. "But tell me, why go north first?"

"I *did* tell you. Because my uncle's there."

"And your people? Are they in the north? Or in Miromara?"

"In Miromara, but—"

Vrăja nodded. "Precisely. You are fleeing too, child. From that which scares you most."

"That's not true! Cerulea is occupied. I can't go back to it without my uncle's help."

Vrăja gave her a long look. "You treat rumors as certainties. Your mother was badly wounded. Your uncle and brother are missing. Yet you speak of all three as if they are alive and well and just waiting for you to find them at any second. How will you face that which is Abbadon if you cannot first face your own truth?"

Serafina looked at the floor. Vrăja's words angered her. But more than that, they cut her. Deeply. Because they were true.

"You fear you will fail at the very thing you were born for," Vrăja said. "And your fear torments you, so you try to swim away from it. Instead of shunning your fear, you must let it speak and listen carefully to what it's trying to tell you. It will give you good counsel."

Serafina picked her head up. "But all I do is make mistakes, Baba Vrăja. I couldn't help my father. I couldn't save my mother. I trusted people I shouldn't have. I went shoaling and got Ling caught in a trawler's net. I couldn't even convince Astrid to stay." Serafina blinked back tears, then said, "My mother wouldn't have made *any* of those mistakes. She's better than that. I'm not like her. I'm not like you."

Vrăja laughed. "Not like me? I should hope not! Let me tell you about me, child. About two hundred years ago, the old obârşie was dying. The elders came to fetch me so she could tell me all the things I needed to know. I was so scared it took the elders an hour to coax me out of my room. One is not born knowing how to lead; one learns."

"But Baba Vrăja, I don't have time to learn," Serafina said. "What's happening in the waters—right now—is life or death. My people, my friends . . . they deserve the best leader they can get. Not me."

Vrăja threw her hands up. "If you wish to be the *best* leader, I cannot help you, for there is no such thing. We all make our mistakes and we all must live with them. If you wish to be a *good* leader, perhaps I can. Listen to me, child, Astrid swam away because she does not believe."

"In Abbadon? How can she not? She saw him. Fought him. We all did."

"No, in herself. Help the others believe, Serafina. Help Ling believe she can break through the silences. Help Neela believe her greatest power comes from within, not without. Help Becca believe the warmest fire is the one that's shared. Help Ava believe the gods *did* know what they were doing. *That's* what a leader does—she inspires others to believe in themselves."

"But *how*, Baba Vrăja?" Serafina said helplessly. "Teach me *how*."

"Serafina, can't you see?" Vrăja said. She reached across her desk and took her hand. "By first believing in *yourself*."

FORTY-SEVEN

THE RIVER WITCH Magdalena looked at the spidery crack Neela had just put into the cave's wall and shook her head.

"You're dead. You missed him by a mile," she said. "And then it was his turn. And he *didn't* miss."

Neela wiped a drop of blood from her nose.

"Try again."

"She's bleeding," Serafina said. "She needs a rest."

Serafina was sitting on the floor of an empty cave the Iele used for spell practice, recovering. Neela, Ava, and Becca were with her. Ling was with Abbadon, where she'd spent most of the last four days.

Before Neela's turn, Magdalena had made Serafina cast an *apă piatră*, an old Romanian protection songspell in which she had to raise a wall of water ten feet high, then make it as hard as stone in order to shield herself from an attack. She'd held it up for a full two minutes, but the effort had left her with a blinding headache.

"Here," Magdalena said now, handing Neela a cloth for her nose.

"You're pushing her too hard," Serafina protested, worried about her friend.

"Abbadon will push her even harder," said Magdalena.

"It's okay, Sera, I'm good. Let's do it," Neela said, stuffing the bloody cloth in her pocket.

Magdalena swam a few feet to the right of the crack. She picked up a rock and scratched a hulking figure with horns and a big ugly face on the wall, then drew an *X* in the middle of its forehead. "Right there," she said, tapping the *X*. "Focus."

Neela, looking at the cave floor, nodded.

"Bring it, baby merl!" Ava called out.

"Right between the eyes, Neela," Becca said.

"Focus, dragă," Magdalena said.

Neela picked her head up. She fixed her gaze on the *X*, and started to sing.

> *I summon to me*
> *rays of light*
> *And make of them*
> *a weapon bright. . . .*

As she did, light leapt toward her from the room's lava globes. She caught it and whirled it into a ball, just as she always did when casting a fragor lux. But this time, she made the ball smaller, tighter, and harder. Just as Magdalena had taught her.

> *Magic, help me*
> *Fight the dark,*

Guide this missile
To its mark.

With a loud cry, she launched the frag as hard and fast as she could. It hit the wall with an explosive impact. Everyone ducked as shattered rock flew through the water. When the silt settled, there was nothing but a deep hole where Abbadon's head had been.

"Excellent!" Magdalena shouted. "Well done!"

"That was *amazing*!" Becca said.

Neela smiled. A bright gush of blood burst from her nose.

"Neela!" Serafina cried. She swam to her friend, pulled the cloth from her pocket, and pressed it to her nose. "That's it. You're done," she said. "The magic is supposed to explode Abbadon's head, not your own. Come and sit down."

As she watched Neela pinch her nose, Sera thought how right Vrăja had been—they *were* stronger when they were together. But their new powers took a toll. Headaches and nosebleeds were only part of it. The hard training they did together also gave them bruises and cramps. Ava had been sick to her stomach several times. Ling's broken wrist started paining her fiercely. They were all exhausted. Magdalena, who would become the next obârşie, was helping them develop the powers passed down by their mage ancestors, and teaching them some old Romanian spells of the Iele. There was much they had to learn if they were going to fight Abbadon and too little time in which to learn it. Magdalena didn't give them many breaks.

"Becca, you're up next," she said now. "Sing a good strong flăcări spell. Call up some wrasse-kicking waterfire."

Becca rose and swam to the other end of the cave. She positioned herself so that she was floating just inches off the cave floor, then began to songcast.

> *Whirl around me*
> *Like a gyre,*
> *This I ask you,*
> *Ancient fire.*

Faint, flickering fingers of waterfire snaked up out of the ground in a circle around her, summoned from the earth's molten core.

Magdalena snorted. "You call that waterfire? Those flames couldn't heat a teapot. You're. Not. *Focusing.* You have to be able to call the fire every time you need it. What happens if Abbadon's advancing on you and you can't make the fire come? You die. Do it again," she said.

Becca took a deep breath and started over. Her voice was louder now, and more forceful.

> *Whirl around me*
> *Like a gyre,*
> *This I ask you,*
> *Ancient fire.*
> *Hot blue flames,*

Throw your heat,

Cause my enemy

To retreat.

As the last note left her lips, there was a loud *whoosh*. The waterfire shot up in a roiling orange column all the way to the top of the cave. Becca was lost inside it.

Magdalena cupped her hands around her mouth. "Becca? Becca, can you hear me? DIAL IT BACK!" she shouted.

All at once, the fire collapsed, its flames sinking back into the earth. Becca was still floating slightly off the ground. She looked dazed. Her curls were singed. Her dress was scorched. She'd burst a small blood vessel near one eye.

"Your powers grow by the hour," Magdalena said. "Unfortunately, your mastery of them does not."

"She needs more time. We all do," Serafina said.

"You don't have it. And I can't give it to you. What I *can* give you is help channeling your magic, if you want it," Magdalena said crisply. "Ava, you're next! I want you to cast an ochi just like you did yesterday. I want you to hold it and then go right into a *convoca*, so you can show it to the others. Do you think you can do it?"

Ava nodded.

Serafina knew the ochi was a hard spell to cast. It was what the Iele used to watch Abbadon. It required that a *gândac*, or bug, be planted near the person or thing the songcaster wished to observe in order to catch the spell and hold it there. Shells, with their ability to capture sound, worked best. They'd all tried casting ochis. Serafina had only been able to see around a corner. Ling had been able to see into Vrăja's study. The obârşie had looked up from her desk, amused, and waved. Neela and Becca had seen the Malacostraca.

Ava had been able to see Abbadon by using the same gândac the Iele used—a shell cast of gold that Sycorax had once worn on a chain around her neck. Generations ago, Abbadon had slashed at Sycorax through the bars of the gate, mortally wounding her. His claws had caught her necklace and ripped it off. As it sank through the water, its chain got tangled in one of the crossbars at the bottom of the gate. It hung there still, glazed with ice, unnoticed by the monster.

Today Ava had only been able to hold her vision of Abbadon for about thirty seconds, but Magdalena was amazed she'd done it at all.

As hard as an ochi was, a convoca, or summoning spell, was even more difficult. It was what Vrăja herself had cast to call them here. Magdalena wanted them all to be able to learn it, because it could be used not only for summoning people, but also for communicating with them.

Ava concentrated. Her eyes could no longer see, but her mind still could. Sera wondered what she was going to try to show them. Not Abbadon, she hoped.

"Do you have it?" Magdalena asked.

Ava nodded. "I'm going to try to show you Macapá, my home. I'll use one of the shells on my windowsill as the gândac," she explained.

"Ambitious. I like it," Magdalena said approvingly.

Ava began her songspell.

> *Gods of darkness,*
> *Hear my plight,*
> *Give to me*
> *the gift of sight.*
> *Gods of light*
> *From up above,*
> *Help me see*
> *The place I love.*

Ava was smiling now.

> *A river wide,*
> *A river fast,*
> *I ask you now*
> *To help me cast*
> *A vision clear*
> *To show my friends*
> *My home,*
> *The place the river ends.*

Serafina closed her eyes, waiting for Ava to shift from ochi to convoca, expecting to see in her mind's eye the Amazon River, where her friend had grown up. Instead, she saw herself. A split second later, she heard a voice inside her head. "Sera? Is that you?"

"Ava!"

"Wow! I'm in your head, *gatinha*!"

"This is *weird*, Ava."

"Ava? Sera?"

"Neela?"

"Yes!"

"Hey there!"

"Becca!"

"Yeah, it's me! I can hear you, Ava! I can hear all of you!"

Another voice chimed in—Magdalena's. "Well, the convoca obviously worked, since Ava is talking to us without talking to us, but the ochi is a total fail. You're supposed to be showing us something far away—the Amazon, right?—but all I'm seeing is Sera and she's right next to me!"

"Wait a minute," Serafina said as the image came more sharply into focus. "That's not the practice cave. And what on earth am I wearing?"

The Serafina in the image was clad in armor and riding a huge black hippokamp. She was bellowing at soldiers, moving them into position.

The mermaids soon saw why. On the other end of the field, a fearsome army was amassing.

Ava let out a low whistle. "*Meu deus!* Those are some mad ugly goblins," she said.

"Feuerkumpel," Becca said grimly.

"Sera, watch out!" Neela shouted.

A goblin had crept up behind Serafina. His black hair stood

high in a topknot. He had a sallow face pocked by lava burns, nostrils but no nose, and a mouthful of sharp teeth, blackened by rot. His small, brutal eyes were as transparent as jellyfish. Serafina could see the network of veins running through them, pulsing with brown blood, and behind them, the dull yellow of his brain. Hard, bony black plates, like the chitin of a crab, covered his body. He was carrying a double-headed ax, its blades curved like crescent moons. As the mermaids watched, he raised it high over his head—then swung it.

"No!" Ava screamed. She scrabbled backward on the floor, as if trying to get away from the vision. As quickly as it had come, it disappeared. *"Que diabo!"* she said out loud. "What was *that?*"

"Your gift growing stronger," Magdalena said.

"No way! It's *not* my gift. My gift is sight. It always has been. I can see the truth. I can see what really is."

"No, Ava. Not anymore. Your ancestor Nyx not only saw what is, he saw what will be. He had the power of prophecy. You do too. You just never felt it until now. It's being near the others that's bringing it out."

"So I saw something from the future?" Ava asked.

"I think so," Magdalena replied.

"Great," Serafina said. "Looks like we have a battle with ax-wielding goblins to look forward to. I'm so happy about that. Because, you know, Abbadon just isn't enough of a challenge for me."

"Magdalena!" a voice called from the doorway. It was Tatiana, another one of the Iele.

"Baba Vrăja wants to see you. Right away." There was panic in her voice.

"What's wrong?" Magdalena asked.

"Captain Traho just entered the mouth of the Olt. The cadavru saw him."

"So? He's done it before. It's only a search party," Magdalena said.

"He has five hundred death riders with him. *Five hundred!*" Tatiana said, her voice edging toward hysteria.

"Calm down, Tatiana. He doesn't know where we are," Magdalena said. "No one knows where we are."

"He does now."

It was Ling. She was leaning on the doorjamb, panting. Her face was flushed from swimming fast.

"But how is that possible? Who told him?" Magdalena asked.

"Abbadon."

FORTY-EIGHT

"**I** WAS *SO* WRONG," Ling said.

She swam into the room. "All this time, I thought Abbadon was talking to itself," she said. "Monster speaks, like, two hundred languages. And a lot of them are very old forms. That's why it took me so long to see the pattern. I mean, ever try to make sense of ancient Abahatta?"

"What pattern, Ling? What are you saying?" Serafina asked, alarmed.

"I'm saying that Abbadon talks. But not to itself. It talks about *us*. Constantly. I didn't understand at first. It kept changing languages so I couldn't follow what it was saying, but now I can. Here, look . . . I wrote down a lot of its words." She showed them a piece of parchment. It was covered with lines.

"Six children the witch sends to defeat Abbadon . . . Scared little children . . . stupid and weak . . . They will not find the talismans . . . They will die . . . Their realms will fall . . . and Abbadon will rise again. . . ." she read aloud. Then she looked at the others. "It hears *everything* spoken in these caves. It says our *names*. Where we're from. Who our mage ancestors were. What our powers are. It talks about everything we've talked about for the past few

days. About landmarks—the ones Vrăja gave us to lead us here. It talks about the Malacostraca. Because we talked about them and it heard us," she said.

"Oh, no," Becca whispered.

"Look, do you see this word here? *Kýrios*. And these? *Zhŭ . . . stăpân . . . dominus*. They all mean the same thing: *master*. It's talking to Traho, or Kolfinn, or whoever wants to free it. It's telling him *everything*," Ling said.

"Which means he knows where we are," Serafina said, fear squeezing her stomach.

"And how to get here," Becca said.

"If the death riders find the entrance to these caves . . ." Neela said.

"You mean *when* they find it. If Abbadon told Traho about the landmarks—the Maiden's Leap, the bones, the waters of the Malacostraca—then it's only a matter of time."

"You have to get out of here," Magdelena said. "There's a tunnel beneath our caves. It will take you several leagues south of here. Well away from Traho and his soldiers. Get your things and meet me in Vrăja's study." She left then, swimming rapidly after Tatiana.

Fury rose from deep in Serafina's heart, like waterfire from the depths of the earth. It pushed out the fear. Traho was forcing them to flee again. He'd torn her away from her home, from the safety of the duca's palazzo, and from Blu. Now he was tearing her apart from the other mermaids when they'd only just come together.

"She's right," Ling said. "We better not be here when Traho knocks on the door."

"No. Forget it. I'm not leaving. Not like this," Serafina said defiantly.

"But we can't stay," Becca said.

"We'll go, but not yet. First, let's really give Abbadon something to talk about."

"Such as?"

"A bloodbind."

"Whoa," Ling said. *"Really?"*

"Really."

"It's darksong, Sera," Ava said. "It's canta malus."

"These are dark times," Serafina replied.

Canta malus was said to have been a poisonous gift to the mer from Morsa, in mockery of Neria's gifts. The invocation of some malus spells could get the caster imprisoned: the clepio spells, used for stealing; a habeo, which took control of another's mind or body; the nocérus, used to cause harm; and the nex songspell, which was used to kill.

"Outlaws use bloodbinds," Becca said. "So they can never turn against each other."

"Traho has made outlaws of us," Sera countered.

"A bloodbind is forever. You break it, you die," Ava said.

"I know that," Sera said. "I want to show Traho that we mean it. That we're all in. Abbadon called us a lot of things. It's right about one—we're scared. But we're not stupid, we're not weak, we're not children, and we won't quit. I still don't know how we're going to do this. I don't know how to use all my powers. I don't even know how to stop Neela's nosebleed. But I do know this: I will fight to the death with you, and for you. It's time Abbadon and Traho and every single lowtide death rider knew that too."

"I'm *so* in," Ling said.

"Me too," Becca and Neela said.

"And me," Ava said. "When do we do it?"

"Now," Serafina said.

"Where?" Becca asked.

"In the Incantarium. By the waterfire. To make sure Abbadon hears us. Loud and clear."

FORTY-NINE

"**H**EY, can I borrow that? Thanks!"

Ling got the halberd away from the guard with a magnitis spell before he even knew what had happened. As he was blinking at his empty hands, she swam into the Incantarium, ducked under the arms of a circling incanta, and stuck the weapon's axlike blade through the waterfire. Serafina and the others followed her into the room. Baby swam behind them.

"Hey! Hey, blabbermouth! Wake up!" Ling yelled, poking the rippling image of the Carceron.

"Great Neria, what are you doing?" an incanta shouted. "You'll get yourself killed!"

"It's a strong possibility," Ling said. She peered at the Carceron's gates. There was only darkness behind them. "Hey! Are you listening, you sorry sack of silt?" she shouted. "Then listen to *this*! We're doing a bind. A bloodbind. You hear that? I said, a BLOODBIND, monster man! Tell *that* to your boss!"

She backed away from the waterfire and waited. Serafina felt her heart slamming in her chest. At first there was only silence, but then they could hear a low growl. A few seconds later, something moved in the darkness. An arm shot out from between the bars, and then two more. They pushed through the ochi, through the water, and into the Incantarium. Hands opened like dark, sinister sea flowers; the eyes in the center of their palms stared.

"You watching, son? Keep watching. We'll see who's weak."

Ling swam away from the waterfire and threw the halberd down. The others were waiting for her.

"There you are!" It was Magdalena, breathless. "I'm to lead you out of here and into the tunnel. Baba Vrăja's orders. All of us are to go except the incanti. If we hurry, we can make the Dunărea by nightfall."

The mermaids ignored her. Serafina pulled her dagger from a pocket.

"Didn't you hear me?" Magdalena said. "We've got to *go*!"

Serafina held the dagger in her right hand and turned her left palm up. Without flinching, she drew the blade across her flesh. Her blood spiraled through the water. As it did, she sang. Clearly. Loudly. With everything inside her.

> *Abbadon, your end has come.*
> *This we vow, as chosen ones:*
> *Drop by drop, our blood is binding,*
> *Forever lives and fates entwining.*

Abbadon growled menacingly. More hands appeared. Sera knew they could have struck at her easily. But they didn't. Abbadon wanted to see what the merls were doing. So it could tell its master. *Good,* Serafina thought.

Neela took the dagger next, and sliced her own palm. Her blood rose in the water. As she covered Serafina's hand with her own, she sang.

> *Our spell is strong, and soon our blood*
> *Will turn the tide and stem the flood*
> *Of Orfeo's evil, dark and dread,*
> *That wakes now from its icy bed.*

Becca followed Neela. Abbadon shrieked. It shook the bars of the Carceron.

> *Together, we'll find the magic pieces*
> *Belonging to the six who ruled,*
> *Hidden under treacherous waters*
> *After light and darkness dueled.*

Ava was next.

> *These talismans won't be united*
> *In anger, greed, or deadly rage,*
> *But with boldness, trust, and courage*
> *As we unlock destruction's cage.*

Ling was last. She winced as she gripped the dagger with her bad hand, then cut the palm of her good one. As her blood rose in the water, and she covered Ava's hand, she sang the end of the bloodbind.

We've gathered here from sea and river,
With a purpose brave and true,
We vow to drive an ancient evil
From our home, the vast deep blue.

As the last notes of the songspell rose, the blood of all five mermaids spiraled together into a crimson helix and wrapped itself around their hands. Like the sea pulling the tide back to itself, their flesh summoned the blood's return. It came, flowing back through the water, back through the wounds. The slashed edges of their palms closed and healed. A scar was left on each hand, a livid reminder that each carried the blood of the others now.

Sera felt that blood inside her. She heard it singing in her veins and thundering through her heart, making her stronger and braver than ever before. Neela, Ling, Becca, Ava—they were more than her friends now, they were her sisters, blood-bound forever.

It wasn't over, this quest that Vrăja had given them; it had only just begun. Sera had no idea if any of them would survive the darkness and danger that lay ahead, but she knew they'd give everything they were, and everything they had—even their lives—to defeat the evil in the Southern Sea.

She could see their determination in Ling's challenging gaze, in the defiant tilt of Ava's head, in the way Becca held herself so straight and true, and in brilliance of Neela's glow.

Ling left the group now and swam to the waterfire. Abbadon moved closer to the bars. "Did you get a good look, monster man? Did you see the blood bind?" she asked it. "Go. Call for your master. You have lots to tell him now."

But Abbadon didn't move.

Becca joined Ling. She sang a powerful flăcări. The waterfire flared high and hot, surging through the bars of the Carceron. Abbadon roared. It flailed madly at the flames, then ran back into the prison's depths. They heard its voice grow fainter and fainter, until they couldn't hear it at all.

"You finished?" Magdalena asked. "Because you've *got* to get out of here. We're running out of time."

"They cannot. The tunnels are sealed now. The caves are empty. Everyone is gone except those of us in this room." It was Vrăja. She had a satchel slung over her back and was bolting the doors to the Incantarium. "In the gods' names, why are you still here? You were told to leave."

"We cast a bloodbind. In front of Abbadon. We vowed we would find the talismans, unlock the Carceron, and kill it. The bind can only be broken by death," Serafina said.

"Which may happen sooner than you think if you don't go *now*," Vrăja said.

"How? You just locked the doors!" Becca said.

Vrăja swam to the far end of the room. A tall object rested against one wall, draped in black cloth. Serafina hadn't noticed it before. Vrăja yanked the cloth. It fell away to reveal a looking glass.

"I cast a *baricadă*, a strong blocking spell. It'll hold them off until you escape through the mirror."

The obârşie had just finished speaking when a massive

explosion came from above. Shock waves tore through the water.

"They're here," Vrăja said.

For the first time, Serafina saw fear in her eyes.

"But they were at the mouth of the Olt only minutes ago," Becca said, casting a frightened glance at the door. "It takes longer than a few minutes to get to these caves."

"I daresay this Traho knows how to cast a velo. Most military mermen know how to speed their troops. Into the mirror with you. Hurry."

"Let's go in together," Neela said. "There's strength in numbers."

"No, you mustn't travel together. We cannot afford for all five of you to be taken," Vrăja said.

There was a pounding, sudden and loud. Traho was on the other side of the door.

Serafina knew it was iron, and impervious to magic. He was trying to batter it down.

"Take these," Vrăja said. She dug in her satchel, pulled out vials of liquid, and handed them around. "It's Moses potion, from the Moses sole in the Red Sea. Sharks hate it. Maybe death riders do, too. Here are some quartz pebbles charmed with transparensea spells. And some ink bombs. They are crude, but effective. They've gotten me out of more scrapes than I care to remember."

Vrăja dug once more, pulled out a handful of dead beetles, and gave some to each mermaid. "I had hoped to teach you the secrets of mirror travel, but there's no time. As soon as you're in the silver, rattle these beetles. There are silverfish in the mirror—large, fast creatures who love to eat them. One will come to you. Tell it where you need to go and it will take you. Hopefully you'll be out of Rorrim's realm before he knows you were in. Neela, you first."

"But Baba Vrăja, I'm not ready for this!" she said, pocketing her beetles.

The battering grew louder.

"Go, child!" Vrăja said.

"How will we contact each other?" Neela asked.

"A convoca. The mirror. A pelican, if you must."

Sera threw her arms around Neela and hugged her good-bye. "Don't be scared, Neels," she said. "Nothing, and no one, is more invincible than you."

Becca was next, then Ava with Baby, then Ling. Sera felt as if each was taking a piece of her heart with them. The iron door groaned under the pounding of Traho's troops. She could hear their voices coming from the other side. A hinge came loose with a wrenching screech.

"It's your turn, Sera. Go now," Vrăja said. She held her close and kissed her. "I may not see you again. Not in this life."

"No, Baba Vrăja, don't say that, *please*."

"Godspeed, child. The hopes of all the waters of the world lie with you now. Find the talismans. Kill the monster. Before the dream dies and the nightmare rises."

Another hinge gave way. The door crashed into the room.

"Go!" Vrăja cried.

Serafina leapt into the mirror and the liquid silver closed

around her. She looked back, with tears in her eyes, in time to see death riders flood into the Incantarium. In time to see Traho break the circle.

In time to see Vrăja pick up a rock and smash the mirror.

ACKNOWLEDGMENTS

MY HEARTFELT THANKS to Stephanie Lurie, Suzanne Murphy, Jeanne Mosure, and the whole Disney team for introducing me to Sera and the gang; to Steve Malk for being the most wonderful agent an author could ask for; and to my mother, Wilfriede; my husband, Doug; and my daughter, Daisy, for their love and encouragement, and for always, always being there for me.

GLOSSARY

ABBADON an immense monster, created by Orfeo, then defeated and caged in the Antarctic waters

ACQUA BELLA a village off the coast of Sardinia

ACQUA GUERRIERI Miromaran soldiers

AHADI, EMPRESS the female ruler of Matali; Mahdi's mother

ALÍTHEIA a twelve-foot, venomous sea spider made out of bronze, combined with drops of Merrow's blood. Bellogrim, the blacksmith god, forged her, and the sea goddess Neria breathed life into her to protect the throne of Miromara from any pretenders.

AMĂGITOR Romanian word for *deceiver*

AMPHOBOS the language spoken by amphibians

ANARACHNA Miromaran word for *spider*

APĂ PIATRĂ an old Romanian protection songspell that raises water ten feet high and then hardens it into a shield

ĂPARĂDHIKA Matali word for *criminals*

APATEÓN Greek word for *deceiver*

AQUABA a mer village near the mouth of the Dunărea river

ARATA a spell that allows its caster to manifest in a chosen location

ARMANDO CONTORINI duca di Venezia, leader of the Praedatori (a.k.a. Karkharias, the Shark)

ASTRID teenage daughter of Kolfinn, ruler of Ondalina

ATLANTICA the mer domain in the Atlantic Ocean

ATLANTIS an ancient island paradise in the Mediterranean peopled with the ancestors of the mer. Six mages ruled the island wisely and well: Orfeo, Merrow, Sycorax, Navi, Pyrra, and Nyx. When the island was destroyed, Merrow saved the Atlanteans by calling on Neria to give them fins and tails.

AVA teenage mermaid from the Amazon River; she is blind but able to sense things

AVARUS Lucia Volerno's pet scorpion fish

BABA VRĂJA the elder leader—or obârşie—of the Iele, river witches

BABY Ava's guide piranha

BACO GOGA captor of Serafina and Neela, in league with Traho

BARICADĂ a strong blocking spell

BARRENS OF THIRA the waters around Atlantis, where the Opafago live

BARTOLOMEO, CONTE the oldest and wisest of Regina Isabella's ministers

BASTIAAN, PRINCIPE CONSORTE Regina Isabella's husband and Serafina's father; a son of the noble House of Kaden from the Sea of Marmara

BAUDEL'S the songpearl shop where Becca works as a spellbinder

BECCA a teenage mermaid from Atlantica

BEDRIEËR one of three trawlers that Rafe Mfeme owns

BIANCA DI REMORA one of Serafina's ladies-in-waiting

BIBIC Romanian word for *darling*

BILAAL, EMPEROR the male ruler of Matali; Mahdi's father

BING-BANG a Matalin candy

BIOLUMINESCENT a sea creature that emits its own glow

BLOODBIND a spell in which blood from different mages is combined to form an unbreakable bond and allow them to share abilities

BLOODSONG blood drawn from one's heart that contains memories and allows them to become visible to others

BLU, GRIGIO, AND VERDE three Praedatori who help Neela and Serafina escape Traho

BORU long, thin herald trumpets

CABALLABONG a game involving hippokamps, similar to the human game polo

CADAVRU living human corpses, devoid of a soul (see also ROTTERS). The Iele use them as sentries.

CANTA MAGUS one of the Miromaran magi, the keeper of magic (MAGI, pl.)

CANTA MALUS darksong, a poisonous gift to the mer from Morsa, in mockery of Neria's gifts

CANTA MIRUS special song

CANTA PRAX a plainsong spell

CARCERON the prison on Atlantis. The lock could only be opened by all six talismans. It is now located somewhere in the Southern Sea.

CASSIO god of the skies

CERULEA the royal city in Miromara, where Serafina lives

CHILLAWONDA a Matalin candy

CIRCE a witch who lived in ancient Greece

CLEPIO a malus spell used for stealing

CLIO Serafina's hippokamp

CONCH a shell in which recorded information is stored

CONFUTO a canta prax spell that makes humans sound insane when they talk about seeing merpeople

CONTE ORSINO Miromara's minister of defense

CONVOCA a songspell that can be used for summoning and communicating with people

COSIMA a young girl from Serafina's court; nickname: Coco

CURRENSEA mer money; gold trocii (trocus, sing.), silver drupe, copper cowries; gold doubloons are black market currensea

DAÍMONAS TIS MORSA demon of Morsa

DAVUL bass drums made out of giant clamshells, played with whalebone sticks

DEATH RIDERS Traho's soldiers, who ride on black water horses

DEFLECTO a songspell that casts a protective shield

DEMETER the ship that Maria Theresa, an infanta of Spain, was sailing on when it was lost in 1582 en route to France

DEPULSIO a songspell that moves objects

DESIDERIO Serafina's older brother

DEVIL'S TAIL a protective thorn thicket that floats above Cerulea

DOKIMÍ Greek word for *trial*; a ceremony in which the heir to the Miromaran throne has to prove that she is a true descendant of Merrow by spilling blood for Alítheia, the sea spider. She must then songcast, make her betrothal vows, and swear to one day give the realm a daughter.

DOLPHEEN the language spoken by dolphins

DRACDEMARA   the language spoken by catfish

DUCHI OF VENEZIA created by Merrow to protect the seas and its creatures from terragoggs

EJDERHA Turkish for *dragon*

FEUERKUMPEL goblin miners, one of the Kobold tribes, who channel magma from deep seams under the North Sea in order to obtain lava for lighting and heating

FILOMENA Duca Armando's cook

FLĂCĂRI a songspell to summon waterfire

FOSSEGRIM one of the Miromaran magi, the liber magus, the keeper of knowledge

FRAGOR the storm god

FRAGOR LUX a songspell to cast a light bomb

FRESHWATERS the mer domain in rivers, lakes, and ponds

GÂNDAC a bug that is planted near a person or thing that a songcaster wants to observe; it catches and holds the ochi spell

HABEO a malus spell used to take control of another's mind or body

HIPPOKAMPS creatures that are half horse, half serpent, with snake-like eyes

HÖLLEBLÄSER goblin glassblowers, one of the Kobold tribes

IELE river witches

ILLUMINATA a songspell to create light

ILLUSIO a spell to create a disguise

INCANTA (INCANTI, pl.) river witch

INCANTARIUM the room where the incanta—river witches—keep Abbadon at bay through chanting and waterfire

IRON repels magic

ISABELLA, LA SERENISSIMA REGINA Miromara's ruler; Serafina's mother

JANIÇARI Regina Isabella's personal guard

JANTEESHAPTA a Matalin candy

KALUMNUS a member of the Volnero family who tried to assassinate Merrow

KANJAYWOOHOO a Matalin candy

KARKHARIAS "the Shark," or leader of the Praedatori

KOBOLD North Sea goblin tribes

KOLEGIO the mer equivalent of college

KOLFINN Admiral of the artic region, Ondalina

KOLISSEO a huge open-water stone theater in Miromara that dates back to Merrow's time

LAGOON the waters off the human city of Venice, forbidden to merfolk

LAVA GLOBE a light source, lit by magma mined and refined into white lava by the Feuerkumpel

LENA a freshwater mermaid—and the owner of several catfish—who hides Serafina, Neela, and Ling from Traho

LIBER MAGUS one of the Miromaran magi; the keeper of knowledge

LING a teenage mermaid from the realm of Qin; she is an omnivoxa

LIQUESCO a songspell that liquefies objects

LOQUORO a songspell that enables a mer to temporarily understand another creature's language

LUCIA VOLNERO one of Serafina's ladies-in-waiting; a member of the Volnero, a noble family as old—and nearly as powerful—as the Merrovingia

MAGDALENA one of the Iele, or river witches, who helps the mermaids master their magic

MAGNITIS a songspell that allows the caster to attract something like a magnet

MAHDI crown prince of Matali; Serafina's betrothed; cousin of Yazeed and Neela

MALACOSTRACA huge crayfish that guard the entrance to the Iele's caves

MARKUS TRAHO, CAPTAIN leader of the Death Riders

MATALI the mer realm in the Indian Ocean. It started as a small outpost off the Seychelle Islands and grew into an empire that stretches west to the African waters, north to the Arabian Sea and the Bay of Bengal, and east to the shores of Malaysia and Australia.

MATALIN from Matali

MEHTERBAŞI leader of the Janiçari

MERL Mermish equivalent of *girl*

MERMISH the common language of the sea people

MERROW a great mage, one of the six rulers of Atlantis, and Serafina's ancestor. First ruler of the merpeople; songspell originated with her, and she decreed the Dokimí.

MERROVINGIA descendants of Merrow

MERROW'S PROGRESS Ten years after the destruction of Atlantis, Merrow made a journey to all of the waters of the world, scouting out safe places for the merfolk to colonize.

MEU DEUS Portuguese for *my God*

MIA AMICA Italian for *my friend*

MINA Brazilian slang for *a female friend*

MIROMARA the realm where Serafina comes from; an empire that spans the Mediterranean Sea, the Adriatic, Aegean, Baltic, Black, Ionian, Ligurian, and Tyrrhenean Seas, the Seas of Azov and Marmara, the Straits of Gibraltar, the Dardanelles, and the Bosphorus

MOARTE PILOTI death riders

MORSA an ancient scavenger goddess, whose job it was to take away the bodies of the dead. She planned to overthrow Neria with an army of the dead. Neria punished her by giving her the face of death and the body of a serpent and banishing her.

NAVI one of the six mages who ruled Atlantis; Neela's ancestor

NEELA a Matalin princess; Serafina's best friend; Yazeed's sister; Mahdi's cousin. She is a bioluminescent.

NERIA the sea goddess

NEX a darksong spell used to kill

NOCÉRUS a darksong spell used to cause harm

NYX one of the six mages who ruled Atlantis; Ava's ancestor

OBÂRȘIE the leader of the Iele

OCHI a powerful spying spell in which the songcaster plants a GÂNDAC, or bug, near the person or thing being observed

OLT the river in Romania where the Iele are located

OMNIVOXA (OMNI) mer who have the natural ability to speak every dialect of Mermish and communicate with sea creatures

ONDALINA the mer realm in the Arctic waters

OPAFAGO cannibalistic sea creatures that lived in Miromara and hunted mer until Merrow forced them into the Barrens of Thira, which surround the ruins of Atlantis

ORFEO one of the six mages who ruled Atlantis; Astrid's ancestor

OSTROKON the mer version of a library

PALAZZO Italian for *palace*

PERMUTAVI a pact between Miromara and Ondalina, enacted after the War of Reykjanes Ridge, that decreed the exchange of the rulers' children

PESCA the language spoken by some species of fish

PORPOISHA the language spoken by porpoises

PORTIA VOLNERO mother of Lucia, one of Serafina's ladies-in waiting; wanted to marry Vallerio, Serafina's uncle

PRAEDATORI soldiers who defend the sea and its creatures against terragoggs; known as Wave Warriors on land

PRAESIDIO Duca Contorini's home in Venice

PRAX practical magic that helps the mer survive, such as camouflage spells, echolocation spells, spells to improve speed or darken an ink cloud. Even those with little magical ability can cast them.

PRINCIPESSA Italian for *princess*

PYRRA one of the six rulers of Atlantis; Becca's ancestor

QIN the mer realm in the Pacific Ocean; Ling's home

QUE DIABO Portuguese for *what the hell*

QUERIDA Portuguese for *darling*

QUI VADIT IBI? Latin for *Who goes there?*

QUIA MERROW DECREVIT Latin for *Because Merrow decreed it*

RAFE IAORO MFEME worst of the terragoggs; he runs a fleet of dredgers and super trawlers that threaten to pull every last fish out of the sea

RAYSAY the language spoken by manta rays

REGGIA Merrow's ancient palace

REGINA Italian for *queen*

RIPTIDE Mermish slang equivalent of *very cool*

RORRIM DROL lord of Vadus, the mirror realm

ROTTER an animated human corpse, devoid of a soul

RURSUS the language of Vadus, the mirror realm

RUSALKA ghosts of human girls who jumped into a river and drowned themselves because of a broken heart

SAGI-SHI one of three trawlers that Rafe Mfeme owns

SCULPIN venomous arctic fish

SEJANUS ADARO Portia Volerno's husband, who died a year after Lucia's birth

SERAFINA principessa di Miromara

SHOALING swimming with schools of fish near the surface of the water, a risky sport for merpeople

SHOKORETH Arabic word for *deceiver*

STILO a songspell that makes spikes sprout out of a water ball

SUMA Neela's ayah, or nurse

SVIKARI one of three trawlers that Rafe Mfeme owns

SWASH Mermish slang; a shortened version of *swashbuckler*, suggesting a flamboyant adventurer

SYCORAX one of the six rulers of Atlantis; Ling's ancestor

SYLVESTRE Serafina's pet octopus

TAJDAR Foreign Secretary of Matali

TALISMAN object with magical properties

TAVIA Serafina's nurse

TERRAGOGGS (GOGGS) humans. Before now they haven't been able to get past the merpeople's spells.

THALASSA the canta magus, or keeper of magic, of Miromara; addressed as Magistra

TĬNGJŬ Qin word for *jerk*

TORTOISHA the language spoken by sea turtles

TRANSPARENSEA PEARL a pearl that contains a songspell of invisibility

TREZI the songspell used to turn a corpse into a cadavru

TRYKEL AND SPUME twin brother gods of the tides

TSARNO a fortress town in the western Mediterranean

TUBARÃO Portuguese for *shark*

TUDO BEM, GATINHAS? Portuguese for *Everything well with you, girls?*

VADUS the mirror realm

VALLERIO, PRINCIPE DEL SANGUE Regina Isabella's brother; Miromara's high commander; Serafina's uncle

VELO a songspell to increase one's speed

VITRINA souls of beautiful, vain humans who spent so much time admiring themselves in mirrors that they are now trapped inside

WATERFIRE magical fire used to enclose or contain

WAVE WARRIORS humans who fight for the sea and its creatures

YAZEED Neela's brother; Mahdi's cousin

ZEE-ZEE a Matalin candy

ZENO PISCOR traitor to Serafina and Neela, in league with Traho

COMING IN 2015:

Waterfire Saga Book Two

ROGUE WAVE

VENICE

Lagoon
CERULEA
TSARNO

MIROMARA

MIROMARA

MIRON